Virgins, Guerrillas & Locas

Gay Latinos Writing on Love

Edited by Jaime Cortez

Published in the United States by Cleis Press Inc.
P.O. Box 14684, San Francisco, California 94114

Printed in the United States
Cover design: Scott Idleman
Cover art: Tino Rodriguez
Text design: Karen Huff
Cleis Press logo art: Juana Alicia

First edition
10 9 8 7 6 5 4 3 2 1

"They Say I'm One of Those" by Raúl Thomas is excerpted from *Dicen Que Soy* (Madrid: Betania Press, 1993). "The Last Stand of Mr. America" by Jason Flores Williams is excerpted from *The Last Stand of Mr. America* (San Francisco: Caught Inside Press, 1998).

Cover artist Tino Rodriguez is a painter based in San Francisco. He is represented by Brewster Arts in New York City and Bucheon Gallery in San Francisco.

Library of Congress Cataloging-in-Publication Data

Virgins, guerrillas, and locas : gay Latinos writing on love / edited by Jaime Cortez.—1st ed.
p. cm.
ISBN 1-573-44087-6 (alk. paper)
1. Gay men—United States—Literary collections. 2. Hispanic American gays—Literary collections. 3. Hispanic American Men—Literary collections. 4. Gay men—United States—Biography. 5. Hispanic American gays—Biography. 6. Hispanic American Men—Biography. 7. Love—Literary collections. I. Cortez, Jaime.

PS509.H57 V57 1999
810.8'09206642-dc21

99-043946

This book is dedicated to Diane Felix.
The roots of this anthology can be traced back to you and the crew at Proyecto ContraSIDA Por Vida.
Thank you.

Contents

Acknowledgments

Thanks to the contributors for inspiring, educating, and touching me.

To Joel B. Tan for getting the ball rolling on this project and for consultation on demand. Varsity girls rule!

To all my top-drawer hookers (Joel Villalon, Tisa Bryant, Pato Hebert, Jose E. Muñoz, Jorge Cortiñas, Ricardo Bracho, Marcia Ochoa, and Sarah Patterson) for the edits, advice, and love.

To Adan Griego and Luis Alfaro for the writer contacts and support.

To Cleis Press for backing this endeavor.

And of course, thanks to Felipe and Felisitas Cortez, for loving me so well.

Foreword

José Esteban Muñoz

This book is a brick. But it is not a brick that sinks. It's something else. It's heavy with meaning and love. It feels good in our hands. We can throw it and it will fly in the air with tremendous force. But we need to hold onto it. We can and must use it to build a world of possibility, for this book is a building block imbued with possibility. *Virgins, Guerrillas, and Locas* is a crucial component in a project that we can best understand as world-making. This object that you hold in your hands is a valuable component of a queer and brown world that is still to come, that is off in the horizon yet, nonetheless, is right here and right now. To say that it's still on its way and already here is not a contradiction; on one level the stories and testimonies in this book do announce a future of brown and queer possibility, but on the other hand these cuentos zoom on the incredible power of our own contact with each other.

We do not know ourselves, our passions, our drives, our beauty, and our power until we establish contact with each other. These are stories of contact, narrations that tell us of the world-making drama that unravels when we know each other and see each other, when we understand the incredibly ennobling sense of possibility that our contact engenders. As I travel through these pages I meet fierce sisters/brothers who fill me up, call me out, and make me.

These stories of contact help me think of the first gay Latino man I ever loved. I met Tony in high school, and we hated each other at first. Our suspicion was borne of an instant knowing of each other, seeing our own faggotry in the other's eyes, voice, and movement. Was I that maricon? Distrust faded and I found myself in this brother. The love I had for this twisted cubanito was the kind of love that remade my world, tore it down, and built it up again. Familia expanded beyond mami, papi, and all the others. Family now included the beautiful freaky mirror who helped create me through my own reflection. We flew through Miami in his sputtering beige Nissan and renamed the world. We invented a language, as old as it was new. Our bond pushed against our former reality; through it, we insisted on a spaciousness that could accommodate our queer and colored reality.

We both left the Hialeah lifeworld behind and headed north. I read *This Bridge Called My Back* in college, where I was learning how to be a feminist. I also soaked in the amazing black feminist classics *Homegirls* and *All the Men Are Black, All the Women Are White, but Some of Us Are Brave.* Those books clearly influenced brother Joseph Beam's heartbreaking and beautiful *In the Life* and Essex Hemphill's incredible sequel to that text, *Brother to Brother.* These books had an amazing affect on this scholarship boy as he also soaked up critical theory by white theory masters. Those important anthologies of colored activism and passion helped form me both as a scholar and as a person engaged in the never-ending endeavor that is politics. Yet an act of translation was always in play. Yes, the sistahs of those early feminist interventions stirred me, and I was roused from a long, white, assimilationist sleep by the achingly gorgeous testimonies in the brothers' books. But there was always an act of translation that mediated my access to these key works. The book that would speak directly and acutely to my reality, my politics, was still a long way off. Now, finally, it is here. This book, then, will arm our younger brothers as they come up and come out; it will instantly give important snapshots of bold and brown queer worlds where men love each other and live outside the law.

Books, like people, can provide us with armaments we need to overcome the obstacles placed in our path. The writers in this book are striving to transcend a world where Latinos are either the hot and spicy fetish or the scapegoated alien invader (often both, simultaneously). The world we are writing against is a place where queers are walking targets for countless brigades of zealots whose bids for national prominence are increasingly effective. Furthermore, many who live under the sign "Latino and queer" are also shadowed by economic poverty brought on by a rapidly stratifying class system. The colored queers who are often the urban poor get poorer. Our ultimate resource for survival is ourselves, our contacts. My socio Ricardo Bracho writes about his wishes for his hijito in his moving analysis of the formative father/son bond, *Daddy*. First and foremost he wants to help build the boy strong enough so that he can survive; and his writing, like the writing of all the reconstructed racemen in these pages, will help build us up strong—strong enough to withstand mad drama that we did not author and strong enough to compose our own drama.

Jamie Cortez asked the men who fill out these pages to write about love, and they have done more than just write—they have performed acts of critical, lyrical, and political love. Assembled between these covers are transmissions from lived worlds of struggle, survival, and arrival. These testimonios and cuentos are calls that will reverberate far and wide, calls that depend on the response of brothers who have lived, are living, and will live this sumptuous vida loca. *Virgins, Guerrillas, and Locas* and more are called out and into reality.

Introduction

Jaime Cortez

Queer Latino stories of love have always been with us, crouching on the tips of our tongues, coursing just beneath our skin, burning across telephone lines, and then evaporating. For a long time, however, our stories have lain undocumented, awaiting the happy coalescence of writerly nurturance, artistic organizing, and publisher interest. Early efforts to compile our works met with some success, but never achieved the status and exposure of, say, *Brother to Brother*, a classic of black gay literature. For this reason, we have much to celebrate in 1999. *Virgins, Guerrillas, and Locas* is the second queer Latino anthology published this year, and a third is on the way. This constitutes nothing less than a literary flowering of great breadth and beauty. It's good to be here.

The first few weeks of work on this anthology were marked by crippling panic attacks. Each morning I rose and found that, overnight, a few more doubts had mushroomed. What makes me qualified to edit this anthology? How do I find enough authors? What if the material is insipid and uninspiring? What *is* the rule for using semicolons instead of colons? As it turned out, only my fear of punctuation was well-founded. The rudiments of a national network of queer Latino writers were already in existence. One writer led me to another, and I soon had a database full of names.

My goal was to be more than a compiler of stories, so I provided the best support I could to those who submitted stories. Nineteen of the pieces in *Virgins, Guerrillas, and Locas* are brand new or never before published, so I went through an average of three or four rounds of edits with each author. Long before the manuscript was compiled, this process paid off handsomely for me. To work with so many talented brothers and to watch their works take on polish with each edit was a privilege indeed.

I asked these men to write of love, because I wished to give them an entire continent of emotion, politics, and themes to explore and document. Their wayfaring has yielded beautifully variegated riches. They approached the subject of love through humor, deeply personal ruminations, ambitious political analysis and fanciful storytelling. Some wrote in the baroque Latin American style, crowning intricate sentences with flourishes and curlicues. Others favored the desert beauty of spare, arid prose that leaves the reader only footprints and ripples by which to track meaning. Some chose to italicize Spanish words; others left them unitalicized—a statement of grammatical resistance.

Amid this diversity of theme, style, and approach, I noted five topic clusters, and I divided the anthology into five sections, entitled *Silences, Virgins, Delirium, Locas,* and *Guerrillas.*

The stories in *Silences* demonstrate that love is not merely a feeling, but rather a communicative act in which words can be misleading or irrelevant, while silences can be all-important in discerning the true contours of relationships. The man learning to love and fuck his deaf boyfriend knows this. Boys groping for an understanding of eerily silent familial splintering know this. Men grappling with conflicted nostalgia, timeworn lusts, and the piercing political truths of their desires know this as well.

In *Virgins,* I gathered accounts of queer boys being broken into the world of love—sometimes sweetly, by doting biker fathers and adolescent boyfriends, other times horribly, beneath the lash of homophobia, self-hatred, rape, and institutional abuse. The writers detail these early wanderings into love, sex, intimacy, and longing with passion, verve, and a sense of humor.

Delirium is a ragged but gorgeous bouquet in which blooms of ecstasy and immolation are tightly bundled by a braided cord of politics, economics, race, death, and longing. Here we see tiny poems as potent as grenades, as well as bluesy accounts of tender infatuation between whores.

La vida loca isn't just for gangsters anymore. The most decidedly "bent" stories have been quarantined in the section *Locas* for close study, for they remind us that sometimes love is best survived through humor and judicious insanity. The picaresque romp of three cha-cha queens on acid through the Bronx Zoo makes this point, and it is driven home by a quirky account of love between a young woman and a famously endowed celebrity crooner from the San Francisco Bay Area. An earthy Virgin of Guadalupe sighting by a cholo junkie and the torrid recounting of a high-drama schoolboy and his muscle-bound lover cap off the craziness.

Guerrillas is the headquarters for stories written by queer Latinos who have snatched some measure of wholeness and happiness from a world designed to deny them both. These reluctant revolutionaries have returned from harrowing forays to share brutally acquired survival tactics. This is tough love indeed. Hear the words of a father/orphan/lover who is finding his way through the dizzying intersections of race, gender, and politics. See how a straight man comes to truth and redemption through the body of a transgender muse. *Guerrillas* closes with accounts of men who confront their howling fear of loneliness and AIDS, to emerge with a battered optimism that is heartbreaking and inspiring.

These are stories of love, and that is nothing new—yet the well-worn theme of love is refreshed anew in the capable hands of these authors. Their stories howl and keen and moan and giggle and coo and whisper and weep, just as we all do when in the mighty arms of that dark angel whose name is Love.

Silences

Joaquín (who thinks his name is Jack)

Jorge Ignacio Cortiñas

On the night my mother left my father, she took things that I have only recently noticed are missing. Things she must have packed tightly into the one duffel bag she carried when she climbed into the pickup truck with the driver's face hidden in the shadow. On the side of the pickup truck it said Vincelli Construction and then it was gone and didn't say anything.

I was at one end of the skinny hallway of our tenement when I saw my mother step out of the bathroom and then noticed that she had on her flower dress, the blue and white one she bought herself because she said it reminded her of windows. She was in a hurry and didn't see me see her as she walked quickly down the stairs with her duffel bag in one hand and her shoes in another. I opened up the window in the living room and saw her come out from under me and then she was sitting in the truck. And then it was just the spot where the truck had been, with other cars passing through it.

My father did not say anything for two days. Then he came out one morning and sat across from my cornflakes and said, Your mother's gone away, like he was talking about bad weather and there was nothing he could do. I kept eating and then I said, I know.

That's when he gave me his talk about how he knew I was going to clean up more and help him. He said that word a lot. Help. He was holding one of his hands in the other and if he let it go it shook without making noise. He said he wasn't going anywhere, that he was staying right here, and then he patted my head and then I felt my insides jump back and then I was watching both of us from across the room. He was never going to be able to see me seeing him the way he was, dried skin under a terry-cloth robe.

Nights after that, I could hear the radio inside my father's room. He kept it tuned to the Spanish station, full of men's voices mumbling in-between songs with a beat slow and sad and horns that held their notes like a three-minute sigh. After he started snoring, the station would switch to static that didn't stop off till he stumbled out in the morning, the bedsheets tangled like an argument behind him.

I was in the kitchen, standing under fluorescent tubes that stuttered, when I heard the door of his bedroom creak open as I closed the refrigerator. His footsteps plodded on the carpeted hallway as I poured out the last splash of milk. He was pissing in the toilet as I rummaged for something else to have my cereal with. The day was gray. I had settled on what there was, the orange juice, and was on my third spoonful when he got to the kitchen door. Out the corner of my eye I could see my father was grinning without showing teeth, the way he did when he wanted to convince me that everything was all right, maybe even special. The swirls of orange juice inside the last of the milk matched the tile on the kitchen floor.

He was standing there and he asked how I was doing.

A minute later he was still standing there. He was grinning and not saying anything, so I said, Fine Dad, fine.

El Sereno

Horacio N. Roque Ramírez

I

Three years ago I stopped by El Sereno to look for you, George. I drove around in the daytime, losing some of my Bay Area whiteness to that nasty freeway sun I miss so much. I frantically roamed around this Los Angeles repository for immigrants, old and new, just to see if something of you and me still remained. Something, like an old, wrinkled wrapper of candy we had eaten together, left over somehow in a sidewalk crack in front of El Sereno Junior High. Or close to the Mazatlán Theater, by Huntington Drive, the one you never took me to. 'Member when I saw you coming out of the theater once with that skinny girl? You were embarrassed, and I wanted to slap you and move her to the side.

I went back, George, driving down Eastern in my old brown car, maybe to play an old video game, Ms. Pac Man, or Frogger. We used to spend all my bus money, and then I'd walk home for more than half an hour, arriving late. I knew my sister would scold me, but it didn't matter since it was you who had made me late. Again. I've gone back almost every four years, like a ritual.

I have never left *this* place, George. Still wondering if you're rumbling through the narrow street—Lynnfield Street, right?—where we'd walk out of school and up that small hill of tiny houses, all their colors faded. I'd be so excited, clutching the six-pack of candy in a small brown paper bag. Corn Nuts. Sunflower seeds. Strawberry and grape flavored Nerds. Rebanaditas. Cheetos. And a fat Snickers bar I could barely wait to stick into my mouth, and bite, bruising its skin slowly, letting the flavor bleed inside. You'd watch my lips smear with melted chocolate, making fun of my carelessness. You probably figured out that it was purposeful, but so what.

I'd carry your Cherry Coke in the other hand, George, 'cos you'd let me, and somehow you always ended up carrying my cheap backpack, 'cos it was heavier, you said, and men do those things. Even little men. You'd always look inside of it and make fun of the order in my world: pale yellow Pee Chees for all my classes, with paper filed inside. All my textbooks carefully protected with brown paper grocery bag covers that turned fuzzy the more you caressed them during the school year, until they wore thin and ripped between your fingers, all that knowledge spilling on the ground. You were the first to see my report cards at school, reminding me that I could never get an "A" in biology. I think you saw that mark of "imperfection" as bridging us in some common cause, that "B" next to your "C"s, bringing us that much closer.

We'd get so fucking high on sugar and salt, making passionate love to our candy. I waited patiently for the lesson plan of the day, and we both understood that the candy was my contribution for your services rendered. Sitting so close, sharing sugared junior high breaths in your bedroom, that walk-in closet turned safety zone for you to invite me over and over, so many afternoons ending up getting your sheets wet and dingy. I remember when you asked me if anything had ever come out, pointing to my crotch.... I didn't know what you meant, but it felt real good to be asked, in English, if I knew something about me, and I understood pretty well, especially after you modeled it for me.

With your clothes hanging in that tiny space, George, all dark fabrics caressing my face as we chewed and swallowed and gulped. Your blue jacket with the hood, zipped all the way up when you wore it. I'd nervously follow the metal teeth with my eyes all the way from your neck to the thick knot of your drawstring. The sweatpants I was afraid to start feeling my way through every time, but every single time I did. The caps you wore on Fridays when you were especially flirtatious with those bad-ass, made-up, up-and-coming cholitas, como Enriqueta—la cara de chancleta, recent immigrants too, pintadas como payasas. I wondered how *they* were able to "translate" with their boys. Did they get *better* private lessons than I did? Better oral history and ethnographic encounters? Were they too following the Five Easy Steps to a Better Chicano English for Centroamericanos, the one you were patenting, and practicing so much on me?

II

I could not leave that place, George, stuck those first months after I got here. New language, new food, new people…and having to get undressed in the locker room during P.E. How could people do that? That was too much, exposing myself like that in front of so many strange guys, comparing foreign parts so early on. I was *glad* you were on top of this drama too, teaching me how to steal those thin, clean white towels from the locker room to give to the shower check guy at the exit and leave the gym as I went in, fully clothed and without letting anyone see me. Early bathhouse etiquette and secrecy, learned at age twelve and refined in my twenties. The idea then, of course, was that only *you* could see me, in another place and away from their eyes.

I have never wanted to leave *this* place now, driving back to see if there's anybody left. Like Mr. Mirales, el argentino from homeroom. He knew that you'd assigned yourself the task of giving me campus tours during second period, but smirked and lifted his thick eyebrows when he saw you standing too close to me, leading me out of the classroom, grabbing my hand firmly. He knew you were to be my Ambassador of Goodwill, translating this new world of El Sereno Junior High for me. I'm sure he wanted to know more about us.

Remember the end of second period? Nutrition! We'd all dash to the front of the line in the cafeteria, the whole goddamned brown mass of dark-haired students running for breakfast. I always felt sorry for the ones who had second period in the school's makeshift classrooms, those bungalows far away by the track, the ones that creaked when it was windy. They were far from the cafeteria, so they always got the worst grilled cheese sandwiches. I'd always be one of the first to get to trade those faded Globe, Inc., meal tickets for an orange juice, a tiny carton of milk, and that smelly L.A. Unified School District coffee cake, soft and moist and crumbly. A complete breakfast for free!

You always took my milk—no, actually I let you have it. ...I never liked it, and your wet lips guzzling down the little carton in less than two seconds made me wish I had more meal tickets. Your stocky brown body fattening up with that white shit. Fuck! I've always dreamt of running to you and hugging you tight as you swallowed it all, squeezing your tummy just right so that you could burp up a few of those calcium bubbles in the air and let them pop on your face as they landed. And I could then lick some of it. An even trade, I thought: my milk for a little taste of your gut, the place you laughed so hard from *every time* I mispronounced all the words you tested me on. "Say, 'You're a BITCH,'" you'd say, "not a 'BEACH.'"

I would have liked that a lot: to go inside, dig some of that gut up and taste you, get you stuck in me for good; my own private opportunistic infection, maybe, with no treatment, lingering there and never quite leaving.

III

Wherever the fuck you are, George, can you smell me back to your own memory? Do you taste our history the way I can still taste you if I try real hard when I get on my knees? In that moment, George, I sniff you back to where we left off, between your khaki

Dickies and my cheap, green, seventh grade shorts, the ones you'd make fun of too, 'cos no self-respecting studious vato-in-training, you said, wore shorts. But *I* didn't know what school was not made for, so I just went along with the same clothes I knew from where I came.

I let you make fun of it all, even the whole immigrant experience, which you found so funny. And someone who had come from a real war kind of excited you. I guess you didn't think about the Vietnamese or Cambodian students in El Sereno who had that war thing going on for them, too. I guess I was the lucky immigrant you wanted. I was the one who would let you clutch me from behind, surprise me, and mess up my uncombed hair even more with your hard knuckles. And dark-skinned Ms. Guzman (*not* pronounced in Spanish, you'd tell me), she would just look and smile, an obviously lesbian P.E. teacher peeking at a not-so-obvious lovers' private time together, what the school grounds were really made for.

You knew that's what I wanted but never demanded openly: play-time commitment from you by the benches, a drill of unspoken vows under the basketball court hoops. A power relationship in the classic sense with you putting down my foreign tongue, a bit of linguistic demolition of the Other, only to build me up again with your home invitations. Though racked with guilt for desiring you, I accepted because I *knew* that you wanted to play too, that those painful two-seconds-too-long bear hugs you gave me let your sweet sweat mix on purpose with mine. Both of our bodies in quick friction with just enough force to bring that nice pain; I just knew you were smiling. I'd always break out in sweat from being too close to you in public.

Your arms smelled like clean sweat, George, with a hint of the Old Spice you stole that didn't match your age, height, or hair growth. But, fuck, I loved you for that too, for taking me back where my uncles once were, en las playas d'El Salvador, playing and drowning in the sun-soaked sand, with the men gargling agua de coco fresca y aguardiente, and my uncle with his Old Spice scent. My still-blond hair shining with the rays of the sun, and my uncle running his fingers through it, making fun of its non-Salvadoran shade—pelo canche, he'd scream and laugh, con cariño de tío.

The first thing I did when I moved to Oakland was to buy my own bottle, my first (and last) Old Spice. And I didn't care if the Fruitvale Walgreen's carried only the one that smells real fake, way too pretty to remind me of you or my uncles, an artificially produced smell of talcum powder. I thought I was supposed to get manliness in a bottle—con el agua y la carne del coco y licor y arena negra—to splash on my face and irritate my pores after a shave, a fast-and-rough cure to stop the bleeding from the nicks.

See, you never taught me how to shave either, George, just like you never finished your Chicano language instruction. I always thought that I'd see you shave one day, fighting my way into your cramped bathroom to observe the ritual. But you'd never let me get *too* close and get between you and the mirror, to lick the tiny shaved hairs dripping from the edge of the razor, running down your fingers, down your neck, the tiny white river of foam carrying your tiny black hairs, flowing down your skin to your nipple, the left one. Is that what you look like now, George, what you do now?

IV

The last time I went to Cuffs I looked for you in the darkness. One Thursday night, during a Christmas break from school, I found Latinos inside. There must have been at least a dozen half-drunk but very familiar shadows. That made me happy. And I thought, damn, this is nice...too nice almost, but I had to pretend not to be so fucking overwhelmed with so much so fast. I went to heaven that night, George. I forget with whom or how many, but it *did* smell like heaven, with underarms and nipples and rings you recognize with your tongue, and belts and button-flies half-open, and arms stretched up and out to share in the desire of men together, nondenominational and noncommittal, and the memory of you everywhere. Strangers, histories, and needs drowning my recollections of you.

When I left with him that night, we drove up a hill, in silence. After going inside my apartment, we didn't waste any time, just like you never did. "Get what you want and get it fast," you used to say. I lay on top of him, pinning his arms down and far apart, sniffing him before the fuck, pouncing with my mouth to lick that crest above the legs, where the body breaks, where you can talk and you can dig with your tongue until you feel the skin quivering too fast to handle, and you finally feel your way through his ass, opening, your fingers doing the loving. *We* never did that, George, not like that.

I thought that you'd be the one still helping me make sense of the whole madness. It should've been you helping me understand the differences between relationships, marriages, fags, and fucking. It should've been you closing your eyes, thickening, falling back on my sofa in that cold Silverlake apartment. And then leaving. That's all your fault. Not telling me enough in time. And still, even with all the beer, over and over, I haven't lost your scent.

Before I started wanting to forget El Sereno, I went back one last time, and then I just had to give up. I took the bus, the 256 line that worked its way through all those L.A.s I knew: Pasadena, South Pasadena, into the real L.A., El Sereno, City Terrace, East L.A., almost into Alhambra. Leaving my newly acquired San Gabriel Valley suburbia, I had two transfer tickets and a perfectly decorated pineapple upside-down cake, with a whole maraschino cherry in the center of each Dole pineapple slice. I was proud of my first cake, at age thirteen, even if my sister and father maybe felt there was something funny going on in the kitchen. Something odd about a dedicated immigrant nerd not focusing enough on his algebra homework, or on his first non-ESL prepositions test, to run into the kitchen every five minutes to stick a knife into the center of the cake, until it came out clean. All that drama just to make sure the brown caramelized sugar was just right, for you, George, so that you could taste some more of my tropics.

I have never, *ever* been more excited to travel on the RTD for that long. With that confected beauty held carefully inside a paper bag on my lap throughout the entire ride, I thought I had deciphered the address you wrote on my yearbook, small enough for no one else to notice, next to the friendship wishes and Keep In Touch's from my entire eighth grade ESL posse. I never even asked you if you were mad that I had stopped depending on your lessons once I became part of that first-ever ESL Honors class, and was featured in the local paper with the five other carefully selected Future English Speakers of the World from El Sereno: two Mexicans, one Chinese, one Vietnamese, and that loud Hondureño I was embarrassed to share my Central America with. I know you moved, but that was mean: not to guide me back exactly where I wanted to go. Did you even doubt that I'd return? Was it emancipation that fucked it up? Did you get tired of my war stories without dismembered family members involved? Or did I learn too fast for you? Did you yourself fuck it all up by getting that close that fast, showing me that much?

By the time I left El Sereno for good, not by choice but through family circumstance, I was building a nice big space for me and me only. All my books fit in there, maybe a couple of friends, my sweaty hands, and my growing collection of world stamps that let me escape it all, a never-ending geography to help the landless. But that was it. No more special friendships, no more assimilation games or natives to talk to; I could not play that again. I got fucking sick of the refugee-and-rescuer game after a while, of disclosures and explanations. I have given up on translations, especially my own. See, it's not that I'm still stuck, George, unable to move on and forget you. It's that after a while, I got tired of leaving, and leaving, and leaving.

Boots

Joel Antonio Villalón

Almost all the boys wore boots to church. I remember the church as low and narrow with clerestory windows lining the two long sides. The walls were plastered white and the floors painted a forest green. We faced Christ hanging behind the altar while he looked to the sky. Black blood. Black nails. Black thorns. The weight from his stone body hung limp.

Back then, Father Humphrey made the children sit in the first three rows, girls to the left of the aisle and boys to the right. If you arrived late for mass, which my family always did, you sat in the front row. If you sat in the front row, there was no soft place to kneel, because the padded kneelers lowered from the back of the pew in front of you. Kneeling and standing and kneeling and standing was a slow torture in itself and an incentive for us kids to want to arrive early to mass. But what good is any incentive if your parents were not about to be hurried anywhere?

We walked into church, late as usual, but mass hadn't started. Jito and I sat up front, while Marisa sat across the aisle from us with two other girls.

Forty-five minutes into mass, after kneeling for three prayers, watching the cups rise, hearing the bells sing, we knelt again as the priest prayed to God.

...through Jesus Christ your Son....

As he continued, Jito and I started looking at each other sideways...*grant us peace and unity*...shooting sidelong glances at

Marisa, who did the same with us. *Remember Lord, your people....* She sat at the end of her row, and Jito sat at the end of ours, so that they could almost touch if they leaned and reached across the aisle. I looked at Jito...*we offer you this sacrifice*...and he at Marisa...*he took the bread*...and she at both of us. Our eyes moved from side to side faster and faster, our knees throbbing.... *Do this in memory of me...Amen.* Thank God Almighty.

The pews creaked from bodies rising and settling. We beat the dust from our slacks and sat rubbing our knees, relieved. Jito's feet didn't quite reach the floor, and he elbowed me and pointed downward. The tips of his boots were curled like Aladdin's shoes. Marisa saw this the same time I did, and we three started giggling. I elbowed him, and Jito snorted. Noises erupted from his nose, which only made me laugh harder. I bit the insides of my cheeks hard to stop this feeling I couldn't control, when Father Humphrey slammed down his hand from high above his head, "JITO AND JUNIOR MONTERO! AM I GOING TO HAVE TO TALK TO YOUR PARENTS AFTER MASS?" The pews stopped creaking. I heard people stop breathing. "LOOK AT ME WHEN I SPEAK!" I was biting my tongue, "LOOK AT ME WHEN I SPEAK TO YOU!" Heaving, I looked up at his bright, red face with the crucifix looming behind him. Ricky, the altar boy, stood beside him, his hands together at his chest. They glared down at us. "IT'S AS I WAS SAYING BEFORE. THERE WAS LUCIFER THE ANGEL AND LUCIFER THE DEVIL...AND ONLY THE DEVIL WOULD LAUGH IN THE HOUSE OF OUR LORD. Only Lucifer would laugh in the face of God." The wrinkles on his forehead quivered. He continued his stare, raised his hands high above his red face, and whispered, "Let us pray."

"Remember," my daddy said that day, "it's you who's to set Jito an example."

"But what about Mari?" I said. "She's older than me."

"I've watched and seen Marisa set a good example for you. Now it's your turn to set an example for Jito. Remember, if you read, then he reads. If you fight, he fights. You are his teacher. Jito will learn from you."

"But I like to fight."

"Then teach him how to protect himself. Like a man."

"And I hate to read. I'd rather paint."

"Then teach your brother how to draw."

His head was resting on his palms staring at me when I awoke, and his lips moved in the darkness when I fell asleep. On our best days, Jito, our neighbors, and I walked to the playground and climbed the big oak tree whose octopus arms spread so long and heavy they rested on the ground twenty feet away. We sat on the branches looking at the giant wall of bougainvillea to our left and to the stuccoed white church to our right. The red and orange and gold of the bougainvillea burned against our dusty, thorned landscape.

If we turned and faced the field behind the playground, we could see, over the corn and beyond the mesquites, the water tower miles away in Nopalitos. But usually, we faced our street and little wood houses. The kids below spun tops. We felt the rhythm of the branches from the kids swinging from the tires. Some days, there'd be twenty, thirty kids playing on the ground and fifteen kids sitting in that tree, singing and yelling as the wind blew us back and forth and up and down, we clung to those branches for dear life. Gasping, I held my breath between words with my eyes opened wide, because I knew the wind could throw us away.

"Momma, why does Mari get her own room?"

"She has no sisters, Junior, you know that."

"Well, she can have Jito, right? He's kinda like her sister."

"Jito's not a sister, but your brother."

"Why should I have to share with him? He never leaves me alone. And I'm an old guy. I want my own room."

"Then you're lucky to have a friend just like him, right? Someone who likes you like that. And to think, your sister's gotta go to other people's houses if she wants to play."

"She plays alone in her room whenever she likes. She shuts her door, and she won't let me in."

"Listen, when I was a girl, no one lived around for miles. Our house had two rooms. And I had to play with Tía Noelia or your Tío Freddy, 'cause no one else lived near us. We had no choice. Here, you have friends up and down the street. You have fields behind the house to run in, day in day out. When I was a girl, we only had our house, and when I wanted to be alone I climbed on top of the water tower. Or our roof. Or the outhouse, if I wanted total privacy. Nobody was gonna follow me there. You're lucky that you have a room to share with only one person. Have you thought of that? And with somebody who likes you so much. Yes, I'd say that Junior's a lucky, lucky boy."

"But he never ever leaves me alone."

"If you want to be alone, climb on top of the house like I used to. Simple as that. Marisa complains about not having a sister to play with, and I tell her she has two brothers. And you complain about having a brother. Maybe I should dress Jito up in a wig and stick him in Marisa's room, then everyone would be happy."

"That's what I said we should do! Let Jito sleep in Marisa's room. Momma, he wouldn't mind sleeping in her room. He likes her room. He plays with her stuff all the time."

"Pues, maybe instead we should put the wig on you, and you could do the dishes and peel the papas while Mari and Jito both play outside. Would you like that, mijita? I think you would look muy chulita with your hair long."

"I'm not a mijita."

"But you want Jito to be a mijita, isn't that right? How do you think that makes him feel?"

"I only want him to leave me alone sometimes in my room."

"Then talk to Jito. Then let him talk to you. You listen to what he says. Then you talk, and you listen some more. Then later, after you've talked and listened to where you can't talk and listen no more, let me know what the two of you decide."

Marisa twirled in baton competitions. She took lessons every summer and competed in gymnasiums all over South Texas. Her twirling teacher at one time twirled for Texas A&I many years before. Susie came over almost every day to watch Mari practice. Susie and Jito and I lay on our stomachs in the shade and watched the baton, which first looked like it was walking, then running, then spinning, a solid disc of twinkling lights. While this galaxy floated before us, her long fingers fluttered, and her legs kicked and marched and hopped while the three of us nodded at each other and clapped like they do at the games.

Marisa was a big girl. Not big like round, but big like tall. She tied her wild hair into a ponytail. Her dark, heavy eyebrows were set above her wet, brown eyes. Her freckled skin shone like honey. She stood two fists taller than most boys in her class and could talk up a storm and was so smart no one would argue with her, 'cause she'd whittle them down to nothing in no time at all. Jito and I never yelled at her, 'cause we knew she'd beat the crap out of us if she wanted. She was a year older than me and three years older than Jito and had staked her territory long before we'd crawled onto the scene.

Momma once told me, "You're lucky your sister was born before you, 'cause if you'd been born first, your life as the oldest would've brought you much worry."

"But I am the oldest boy."

"Ahhh, but not the oldest child."

On Fridays during competition season, Marisa, Susie, and my mother made their hair up high, with curlicues hanging down around their faces. Before dawn the next morning, I stared out the front window at Mari glittering in her white shoes and socks and sequined sweater in the light from our Galaxy 500. My mother opened the car door for her, and Mari ducked her head carefully so as not to hit her high hair on the car ceiling. Susie, who didn't even twirl, was dressed exactly like Mari. The headlights backed out of the driveway, and down the caliche road the three hairdos drove.

Well, no matter how expertly Marisa performed at these meets, she never beat the triplets from Victoria. Mari called them las cuatas plus one, 'cause two were identical and the third was a leftover. Their teacher twirled for Texas A&M and not A&I, and the sisters were so good they took turns letting each other take the blue ribbon. This sideshow, as my father called it, went on for years with the other parents screaming at the judges, 'cause their daughters would never and could never win.

Now, Mari's a winner, and if she couldn't win, she could at least quit "at the height of her career," as she would say. Which is exactly what she did. By some miracle from God, after countless promises had been made by my mother to la Virgen de San Juan, she placed second at a meet, and she quit, a silver medalist after cuata number two. My mother flashed two rolls of film while my sister stood on that platform during the medal ceremonies, and Mari said she was blind for almost two weeks. She couldn't see the baton even if she wanted, she told my parents, so why not quit while she was ahead?

When Mari quit, Jito took a liking to her batons. He used them as bats to hit rocks into the field, which was a talent in itself, 'cause the batons were very thin. Sometimes, he stood them in the dirt to create a tent, using a bed sheet and four heavy rocks. Other times, he carried his arm straight and propped the baton like a rifle as he marched from room to room chanting, "One, two...scooby-doo...three, four...shut the door."

Between the batting and the gunning, Jito twirled the baton with his fingers. I never said anything, though I knew I should've. What I would've said, I don't know, but I should've said something, I guess. At first, his movements were clumsy, and the baton fell again and again. But after a while, the baton began throwing off that cascade of light, as if fire sparked from his fingers. With his back to the street, Jito threw the baton in the air as we sat clapping. I sat on the porch during the performance watching the Galaxy 500 slowly creep down the road. "Do it again!" I yelled, "only higher!" And I smiled. The baton sailed past the trees when our daddy yelled from the car window, "WHAT THE HELL ARE YOU DOING, JITO!" The baton fell two feet from Jito's shoes.

"I'm not doing anything."

"Nothing, my ass. Give those things back to your sister."

"She doesn't want 'em."

"Well, they belong to Marisa. Now give 'em back."

"But he's right, I gave them to him."

"If you don't want 'em, THEN GET 'EM THE HELL OUTA MY HOUSE!" and he yanked the baton from my brother's hold, ran into the house and confiscated all of Marisa's batons one by one from under Jito's bed.

"Why do you let him play with those things?"

"Why should I tell him what to play with and what not to play with? I'm not God. And I'm not his father."

"You're not God, but you're his brother, right? Never ever forget that. Have you taught your brother how to fight?"

"I teach him how to protect himself, like you said."

"But have you seen him fight?"

"He fights with me all the time."

"Now listen, Junior. I know he bugs you, but the next time your brother gets angry, let him hit you."

"But he always hits me."

"I know he hits you, but do me a favor and let him hit you hard. As a favor to me. Teach your brother howta hit. As a favor to him, teach your brother howta fight."

Jito asked Momma and Daddy whether or not he could become an altar boy. Of course they were shocked, 'cause they still hadn't forgiven the priest for yelling at us in front of everyone. After mass, my father approached Father Humphrey and in a solid tone told him he had no right to yell at his children before the parish. That the Father should've talked to them in private afterward. My mother then said that to embarrass children like that was not his place in life, and if that's what he wanted from life, then maybe he should think about unbecoming a priest.

So months later, Jito told my folks he wanted to become an altar boy, and they looked at each other, but what could they say? How could they say no?

During the months that followed, I sensed a holiness come over my brother. I saw the way he watched Ricky genuflect before the altar, the way he stared at Jesus hanging on the cross. I never looked up, because he bored me, but I could see that what Jito saw in Christ was like nothing I'd ever seen.

"God, what does snow smell like when it's falling? Like a raspa before the juice? God, why is my head so round and my neck so skinny? God, why is my brother dumber than me?"

"Don't talk about me that way."

"Shhhh," he'd say, "I'm talking to God."

He attended the classes Father Humphrey taught. He practiced genuflecting and bowing with Ricky, and at night, he sat at his desk memorizing prayers from little green books. I'd awaken some mornings to see him standing next to me doing the sign of the cross to my face, saying, "Not to worry, my son, God will forgive you." He knelt every time he walked past Momma's altar in the hallway and rang the cowbell every night before supper.

The four of us sat on the tenth row that Sunday. After that one Sunday, we never sat up front with the other children. Marisa elbowed me, and we awaited my brother's debut. "Aaaaaaaavee Mariiiiiiaaaaaaaa," and everyone stood. I turned to my parents, who looked toward the entrance. White light fell into the room as the door creaked open, and the silhouette of the tall crucifix bobbed over heads making its way from row to row to row, till I could see that little Jito carrying the cross was really not that little and not even Jito, but Bobo from down the road. I looked at Marisa, and she turned to Mom and Dad, who stared toward the rear of the church. Wasn't he supposed to carry the cross today? Mass started, and we sat and wondered where Jito could be. Near the end of mass, my father gave us a signal, and we rose from our knees and stepped to the altar to take the holy bread. The priest looked not at my eyes but at my tongue, and instead of returning to my seat I continued toward the rear exit, and Mari and Mom and Dad filed out the door behind me into the sunlight.

We walked around the church and into the parking lot as we heard singing filter through the walls. We searched the grounds of the rectory and then walked home slowly down the road. From the road and above our roof, we saw Jito in our backyard sitting high in the oak tree above my mother's chair. We ran to the tree's gargantuan base looking up, our hands shielding our eyes.

"Jito," Dad yelled, "what happened?"

"I quit," he said.

"But why?"

The branch swayed, and he continued looking past the tree and the fields. "I got scared."

"Did Father Humphrey say something?"

"No."

"Then who scared you?" Again he moved back and forth. "Jito? Who scared you?"

"I don't know."

"But somebody must've. If you said...."

"God...I got scared of God."

"But God loves you. You know that. There's nothing to be scared of. Come down, Jito. I promise, you won't get scared next time."

"No, I won't, 'cause I quit."

He rocked slowly in the wind.

"But they'll take you back."

"I don't wanna go back."

"I know they'll take you..."

"Don't you hear me?... I said, I quit!"

"Jito, now be careful and get down," my father said.

"I...said...I...quit! Now go away. All of you. Just leave me alone."

We looked at each other, turned, and walked into the house. In our kitchen, we said nothing. My mother lit the stove. My father walked to his chair on the front porch to read the Sunday paper. Marisa ran to her room to change out of her dress. I lay on my bed in my dress shirt and slacks, my head on the pillow, looking out the window watching the oak's arms bend. Perched near the top with his pointy boots curling, my little brother was talking to God.

The next day, the afternoon bus dropped me, Marisa, and the other kids off at the church on my way home. As the bus pulled away, I heard a commotion coming from the playground next door, and I ran across the yard toward the crowd of kids gathered in a circle. In the middle stood Jito across from Ricky, the altar boy, the biggest kid in his grade.

"You don't know who God is." Ricky stepped forward and pushed Jito's shoulder.

"Sissy," he shouted as he pushed.

"God?" my brother said. He turned his head and looked at everyone who surrounded him. The children stood quiet. Ricky dragged his shoe across caliche.

"Step over that, you sissy," Ricky pushed Jito harder. Jito looked around. "Don't you hear me? I said...step over that.'"

"Sissy!" shouted someone in the crowd. Jito's eyes watered. "Sissy!" another yelled. He resembled Marisa then, with his eyes so round and wet, and Ricky pushed again. Jito turned and saw my face in the crowd. His lips began trembling. I pushed my head forward.

"Fight! What are you waiting for? Fiiiight! You're no sissy!"

Everyone turned toward me. His eyes fell to the ground. "Thittthhhy." Ricky spit.

"FIIIIGGHHHHHTTTTT!!!!!! I yelled.

"Aaagghhhh!" Jito dove, and they rolled. "AAAGGGHHHH."

"You like that, don't you?" Ricky pounded Jito's chest. "You sissy, you like that!"

"Hit him, Jito! HIT HIIIMMM!" Blood smeared from his nose.

"Sisssssssssy!"

"Aaaaggghhhh." He kicked. And hit. He spit.

"Hit HIMMM!!!!"

"Aaaagggghhhhhhh!"

And at once, Alex and Mari jumped in and pulled the kicking boys apart. "Sissssy!" Ricky spit. Alex pinned him to the ground.

"Sisssssssy!!!! Sisssssssssy!!!! SISSSSSSSSSSSSY!!!!" my brother yelled.

"He called me 'sissy,'" Jito whispered as Mari pulled him away.

"Why do you care what he calls you? Who is he? An idiot, right? You're gonna fight every idiot you meet?" She wiped his face with her shirt. I ran to where they stood. "Where were you?" she asked.

"He told me to fight," Jito pointed.

She stopped wiping the blood from his nose. "What?"

"He told me to fight."

"You told him to fight?"

"He stood up to Ricky, didn't he? Didn't you see him? He kicked his butt, goood!"

"You stood there and let someone that size hit your brother? You stood there and watched?" She let his arm go. She pushed my shoulder. "You let someone hit him." She pushed me again. "You stood there and watched!" And with both hands, she pushed my shoulders with such force I was thrown on my back five feet away. I didn't lift a hand either to stop her blows or strike back. I took the hits to my chest and kicks to my legs as the children silently surrounded us, and my sister muttered under her breath, "You think it's good for people to fight, do you?"

That night as I lay in bed with my door closed, I could hear my parents yell all the way on the other side of the house. We were bathed and fed and sent to bed, and from under the covers I wished the wind would blow the curtains so that the air would push their sounds down the hall and out through the windows at the other end.

"What do you think Father Humphrey told Mom and Dad?"

"Leave me alone."

"But what do you think he said?"

"Who?"

"Father Humphrey."

"Father Humphrey said nothing."

"What do you mean he said nothing?"

"I was there. He said nothing."

"How could he say nothing?"

"Are you deaf? Can't you hear me? The Father said nothing.... Now leave me alone."

"But how could..."

"I said...leave me alone."

I shut my eyes hard, picturing in my head that scary, skinny line we draw in caliche. The line that curves, we dare to walk. The line we sometimes dare to cross. My eyes saw only that line in the blackness of that night as the three of us listened to our parents in the other room. We passed through that moment…

Oh my God, I love you,

and because I love you,

…with no one to talk to…

I am sorry for all my sins.

…and only I could hear my little Jito pray.

I promise to be good and to sin no more.

Amen.

I Love You Alto

Lito Sandoval

Mike sits on the edge of my bed, bug-eyed like a boy who's seen nudity for the first time. His plump body slouches and leans forward amid the unfolded clothes I've just pulled out of the dryer. He is completely enthralled by the TV news. I wonder why he bothers watching. It's not like his TV. There are no scrolling words highlighted by a blue box. Instead, he is guided by little pictures that float above the anchorwoman's left shoulder. He searches for words: San Jose, gay, hate crimes, deaf. Today the icon reads "earthquake." He turns to me frantically, pointing to the TV while his shoulders shrug repeatedly. He barks an unfinished word each time his shoulders move up, "Wha? Wha? Wha?" I grab our notepad and write out the explanation. *Small earthquake in San Jose. No damage.* As he reads my answer, his right arm drops to his side while his hand spells out the words so rapidly and casually it looks like he is exercising his joints. Then he nods his head in acknowledgment, mouthing a silent "oh" of understanding.

Communication for us is writing notes. I have weekends scrawled on backs of envelopes, flyers, and pages ripped from notebooks of lined paper. They lie scattered on the floor. I sometimes read them to relive the moment of their creation, to cherish our precious limited times together. He can't write worth shit, but I can decipher his dyslexic leanings. I know "I love you alto" on my birthday card, which I keep on my desk, is really "I love you a lot." I correct his misspellings so he'll learn the proper letters.

When I'm not in the mood to write notes, the stage actor in me has to come out. I have to pantomime nouns, verbs. Each sentence is a stream of big gestures and exaggerated faces. This isn't any different from his signing, except for the fact that his movements and gestures are an actual language.

I tell people my lover is bilingual. They assume I'm talking about English/Spanish. I correct them, "No, I mean ASL/English."

After our second weekend together, he bought me a book, *Sign Language Made Simple.* I can whip out a few phrases—the first one being "Do you want coffee?"—but I can't spell. Arthritis has turned my hands into brittle starfish with limited motion. My J's look like E's, which look like A's.

The arthritis does not only affect my hands. I have it all over. There isn't a joint in my body that isn't ravaged and ragged. Some days I just don't want to get out of bed. The simple act of touching foot to ground can be filled with such pain that it creates a burning mental map of all the little bones within. On those days I am a shuffling, 80-year-old man instead of a driven, 31-year-old artist. In some ways I have become used to this, accepted this. But that doesn't make life any more bearable. When I am with Mike, it is more frustrating. Not only can I not finger spell, but acts that as a gay male add value to my worth as a sex partner become reduced. I can't open my mouth wide enough to envelop his fat prick or throw my legs in the air so that he can fuck me while we face each other.

The difficulties of our language and movement became apparent the first time we had sex. I'm used to making noises. Noises are key. They signal pleasure being given/received. My voice shifts, coaxed by a well-placed tongue or finger. When I was about to come, I announced it with a grunt, not thinking that Mike could not hear me. Afterward I felt stupid. When did it become fundamental to announce you were gonna come? Was this a result of watching porn movies where the actors growl out their orgasms? Or did it begin with the onslaught of AIDS—a warning of possible infection if semen should permeate an open surface?

But Mike was not guided by the strength or length of my moans. He looked me directly in the face. This especially became a problem when I decided to let him fuck me. I rolled onto my stomach, spreading my legs. With my face buried in a pillow, he could not see my expressions, could not see my grimace of pain as he tried to ram his cock into me. I turned my head, cried out to him to slow down. He proceeded to enthusiastically thrust into me. Words were useless. I swung an arm around behind me, hit him in his side. He stopped, pulled out. Rolling over, I pretended to write on my left hand with the right; our signal for pen and paper. He looked at me, annoyed, frustrated at the breaking of our spontaneity. I spelled out the necessity of going slower, letting me relax first. We started over again. Even though our union was smoother, it now lacked uninhibited frenzy; a scripted thing.

It is not just communication or physical activities that are impeded. We cannot share sound cues, key signifiers of moments. I remember my friend Albert talking about his ex, Sam. On their second date they were sitting on the floor of Sam's apartment sharing a bottle of cheap wine. Patti Labelle came on the radio. At the same time they exclaimed, "I love that song," which set off their slow, open-mouthed downward fall against each other. From that moment on, it was their song. By coincidence, it came on the radio during our conversation. Albert started crying. I remained silent, touched to witness Albert's neck bravado overcome by his vulnerability. But at the same time, I became jealous. Mike and I will never have "our song." There will be "my song," the one that I heard as we rolled in bed: Al Green's "I'm Still in Love with You." That moment is all mine, and Mike is oblivious. Sure, I could point out to him the moment the song came on the radio, explain its significance to me. I could even tell him when the song was playing, the times we happened to be together. He could act accordingly: oh, our song, let's sigh, hold hands, and do the moony-eye.

A co-worker asked me why I was with Mike, what it was we could possibly be sharing. He explained to me that a relationship had to be more than just sex. He could not understand that our relationship was more than sex. We complement each other. He is the body, I am the voice.

Tomorrow we are going to buy me a closed-caption TV. There's a strange irony in this action. When I initially searched for a new TV, my sister drove me to the giant Whole Earth Access warehouse on the outskirts of Berkeley where her boyfriend worked. He passed me on to a friend of his: "Hey, dude, wassup? Listen, Tony over there can help you. Yo, Tony! Come help this here man." Then he turned all his attention to my sister. They commenced flirting and making plans for the night. Tony gave me a sales pitch, which I was hoping to avoid, and tried to get me to buy a "fresh-out-of-the-box, top-of-the-line Sony with closed captioning." I flippantly stopped him, saying, "Why would I want that? I don't know any deaf people."

I watch Mike watching TV as I finish folding the clothes that surround him. He is not paying attention to me. I creep up behind him, taking care to be stealthy even though he can't hear the clack of my shoes on the hardwood floor. I kiss the back of his neck. He lies back, closes his eyes, and allows me access to the fleshy body. My doughboy baby, masa man, warm and soft. I knead his belly, roll it out with my palms, lift up his shirt, and kiss the smoothness underneath. Then he takes control, careful not to hurt me.

Afterward, we are lying side by side. I point to him and sign "cute." He blushes, holds up his hand. He makes an "L" with his thumb and pointing finger, his pinkie parallel to the pointer. The two remaining fingers stay folded downward. I always considered this an Ozzy Osborne heavy-metal devil sign. In ASL, this means "I love you."

Virgins

They Say I'm One of Those

Excerpt from *Dicen Que Soy*

Raúl Thomas

Only three weeks have passed since I arrived at this place, and it feels as though I've been here much longer, within the walls of this vast, ancient castle.

The lack of sunlight causes the temperature to fall below zero and the intense cold is a constant torment, like a punishment from God. The morning dew now turns into clear frost, which cruelly withers the flowers brought to us by the autumn.

When they wake us, we would dearly love not to take a bath, since the water feels like ice and dries out our skin, leaving us ashen and shivering. I also wish, like everyone else here, that every day was Sunday, so that we could be near the fire that envelops us when we heat the water. With the exception of that day, the rest are the same.

We get out of bed at five in the morning, not a minute before or a minute after. When we hear the first whistle, we open our eyes. By the second, our beds must be made, and by the third we should already be forming lines for the showers. By five-thirty, already bathed and dressed in our khaki-colored uniforms, we go out and form two squads of twenty-five soldiers each in front of the main entrance with its European facade. Then we begin practicing the military drills that our director learned when he was a lieutenant colonel for the 201st Battalion of the Mexican Army, and which now, since he took command of this school, are taught to us daily by his assistants.

To warm up, we begin by sprinting for half an hour. Then, we continue with one full hour of jumping jacks and sit-ups that, besides being good discipline, maintain the muscles through their constant, vigorous motion. We always finish with fifteen minutes of double-time marching, which our instructors believe prevents our muscles and tendons from straining too much. With such intensive military training, I've come to think they're beginning to prepare us for the next war so that we can defend the motherland, and also to ensure that we are not surprised in our sleep by the enemy, as occurred to some Military College cadets, and which I, from the bottom of my feet, hope will never happen since I'm still so little that I don't think I could carry the weight of a rifle.

But if I had to fight for the red, white, and green to preserve our democratic system, I'd do it. And if I die, I would like to die for a just cause. And what better cause than my beloved Mexico?

After the morning exercise, they make us go back inside, since at seven-fifteen exactly we have to enter the dining hall to eat our first meal of the day, which consists of two rolls, one piece of sweet bread, a mug of powdered milk dissolved in hot water, and a bowl of black beans that we devour in the blink of an eye. If anyone is still hungry, they stay hungry, since there are no seconds. This place is not like my home; there, if I wanted to eat a little more, I would, and that was that. But not here. They're a little strange here about food distribution, because there are days when a lot of food is left over, but they prefer to throw it away or feed it to the pigs than to us. According to them, this is done so as not to break our nutritional regimen, and even if we're not satisfied, we have to pretend that we are, and tighten our belts like real Mexicans.

I'll definitely say: they're real bastards.

Before leaving the dining hall, we put our dirty dishes inside a great big plastic bucket that the cooks place at the end of the chipped wooden table reinforced with steel.

When we return, on the back patio we wash our hands and mouths with just a little water—water that we get with an old can tied with twine hanging from a nail embedded in the edge of the trough next to the punishment cell and near the washers, where Saturday after Saturday each person washes his week's worth of dirty clothes.

At seven forty-five in the morning, the whistle sounds again to notify us that it's time for roll call and the announcing of the day's assignments for those under fourteen years of age. We are also sent to classes, which we attend from Monday through Friday. Therefore, those who had a chance to rinse their mouths, great, and those who didn't, too bad, because before the instructor rings that device a second time, we must be in a straight line again so that we can roar as loudly as possible: "Present!" after hearing our name. Pity on those who are daydreaming and don't hear their name and fail to answer! A swift, well-placed kick in the shins awaits anyone who is not paying attention when their name is called. Especially if we're under orders from Señor Isidro, a bastard among bastards and the strictest of the instructors. But our other instructor, whose last name is Dominguez, is nice to everyone.

He doesn't scream at us or overwhelm us during the morning exercises. He's different. He is so kind that just only the other day he told us that if it were up to him, he would just have us go to classes and put in our time until we were eighteen years old so that he could free us from all of this. But unfortunately, he can only follow the director's rules, and even though with all his heart he would like to help us a little more, he can't do much for us.

Today, Roberto Martinez, as his assignment, had to go to the hills and cut grass for the cows and sheep we keep in the stables. Juan Diaz, Marcelo Perez, and Rodolfo Garcia were sent, under the orders of Don Augustine Arevalo, to help harvest the potatoes that are planted on the high land (purchased by him and the director), land to the left of the volcano, where the potatoes grow so big that they look like giant rocks. Poor guys! God willing, they'll get back before night catches them out in the open. You've heard that the mountain devil spirits have appeared and frightened all the country folk up in the mountains. (Hold on while I do the sign of the cross three times, one for each of them, so that nothing bad happens to them.)

Jose Luis Alarcon and Alejandro Arce, together with the two new kids who just arrived yesterday, were assigned to pick pears and apples so that Leonora, the director's wife, could cook them with sugar and cinnamon, for us to eat as dessert on Christmas night, which is soon.

Genaro Martinez, Luis Hernández, and Eduardo Fonseca will bake the bread for this week, including today. Jorge and Apolinar Ortiz, who are brothers and who together stole everything they could in their hometown Soledad de Doblado in Veracruz, will wash everyone's clothes because they didn't wake up on time this morning.

We, the kids in the first to sixth grade, are just waiting for Señor Roldan to start today's class....

On Christmas night, Doctor Cesar Rivadeneyra, mayor of the city and county of Perote, came to visit us, accompanied by his wife. They brought us gifts: a black-and-white television set, a transistor radio (these are now becoming fashionable in Coyocan pink), several packages of animal crackers, and four cases of flavored soft drinks. They had dinner with us and ate the same barbecued meat that Señora Leonora prepared, and they joined us in singing in praise of love and peace, which Father Artemio taught us so that we could sing to celebrate the birth of the holy baby, Jesus.

That same morning, I received my first letter from my mother, in which she advised me to behave as well as I could, to study hard, and to think of her, of my new dad, and of my baby brother (or sister) who was nearing their home now on the wings of the stork. Inside was also a ten-peso bill, folded in half: "for whatever you can use it on, or give it to someone who can go outside and buy you a little candy at least," she wrote at the bottom of the letter, kind of like a postscript. When I finished reading it, I put it in one of my pants pockets, and the following day I gave the money to Armando.

"Here," I said, "take this money, since you get to go outside today. You can buy me two tubes of cacao butter to put on our lips: one for me and the other for you. Look how chapped our lips have become!"

"All right, Witchy," he said, "I'll do whatever you tell me."

Had I already mentioned that the kids nicknamed me "the Raggedy Witch"? No? Then I'll tell you about it.

It happened the same night that they gave us the television set.After we finished eating dinner, they took us to the library and placed the set on a table, tuning it to channel 2, which was showing that week's episode of the "Chocolate Express Story," a program that stars the fantastic Cachirulo. Well, when the evil image of the "Raggedy Witch" appeared on the screen, Marcelo said, loud enough so that everyone could hear, that the evil old lady looks a lot like me—especially her eyes and curved nose. That fucker! Why did he have to say it? Now it's always "Witchy this..." and "Witchy that...," and I'm stuck being the Raggedy Witch.

Armando not only bought what I sent him for, but he also bought a jar of Bell cream and several one-pound brown sugar cubes.

"Thanks, buddy," I said.

"You're welcome, Witchy," he answered.

Without waiting another minute, and to attack the dryness that covered my hands and lips, I opened the cream and immediately spread some over the painfully chapped and shriveled parts of my skin. I then handed it to my friend.

"Go on, you do the same. You see how your lips bleed each time you laugh?"

"Yes," he said.

With both our faces covered in white cream, we looked like red-skinned Indians ready to fight against cowboys. I felt a little strange, but was happy to feel the vegetable grease penetrate my skin and stop the pain from the open sores caused by the harsh winter cold.

Do you know what? The cold gets stronger every day, and though my pants are as thick as the lining of my flannel and lamb's wool jacket, I can't stop shivering for one second. When the wind begins howling from the North Pole, it gets even worse. Despite brisk exercise, it's impossible to compensate for the bitter, erratic weather changes of our volcano-dominated region.

Every day at lunch, they feed us a delicious bowl of soup with vegetables that we ourselves grow in the garden. They add a piece of beef, whose size is determined by how well you get along with the cook. Naturally, a small piece doesn't have the same amount of protein as a large one. They also give us a bowl of black beans and three rolls, one more than in the morning. It could be worse, don't you think?

After lunch comes the formation of the sixty-four bodies and afternoon roll call. As in the morning, we have to answer, "Present!" That way, the person in charge is assured that we're all there, except for the ones who are out on assignment watching over the cattle and the rabbits, whose tiny babies look like blind chickens. Once the two o'clock routine is over, they take us to the library so that we can fulfill our scholarly responsibilities, that is to say, complete our assigned homework and present it to our teachers the following day.

If we finish before five in the afternoon, they let us go out and play for a while. And sometimes, we're allowed to hear the radio that Dr. Rivadeneyra gave to us, which we usually tune to station XEN, which carries the new Kaliman novel *The Incredible Man*.

Our bodies quiver with emotion as we listen, because every day, each new chapter is more and more engrossing and we wish it would never end. I, in particular, like to listen to the adventures of Kaliman, who always fights hand-to-hand and always to the death against the diabolical Count Bartok and his perverse side-kick, Debora. Together, they are the reigning masters of evil nights, along with their zombie servants who have left their tombs to bring panic and grief to the good people of this earth. After listening to all the danger that follows the white-turbaned man and his faithful companion, Solin, I wish I could climb into the radio's warm insides and help our hero fight the evil that fills the horrifically disfigured Count, who always hides in the darkest places of the night or melts into the darkness just before dawn.

"We must struggle against all adversities, my little Solin," he would say to his friend. "We must be victorious in this battle against the evil master of perversity." And yes, believe me, they've survived, even with all the evil that they've come up against on their daily path. I also think that this comes from God, because...can you imagine? Without the help and protection of Our Lord, they couldn't possibly fight with such ferocious strength. And how righteous and beautiful it is that their union should make this world safe from the destructive power of evil forces.

When we finish listening to the story, we cover the radio with the green flannel slipcover that Salvador Jimenez, the tailor, made to protect it from the dust.

Once we finish our schoolwork, we go out to the patio and wait to hear our names called again for the last time that day. From there, we make a line toward the dining room so that we can eat our last meal of the day, which consists of two rolls, another bowl of beans, and a hot mug of coffee...the rest of the week, I don't listen to any other program. Instead, I prefer to go to the library and read. The books are just abandoned there and hardly anyone ever touches them. Only Armando and I remove the ancient dust that covers their fantastic titles. It is so wonderful to read, and there are times when I'm carried away by certain passages and I go flying all by myself toward those places so lavishly described in my book.

And it was precisely here in the library, by means of deceit and threats of "if you don't let us, the three of us are going to beat the shit out of you!" that Genaro, Marcelo, and Ramiro made me drop my pants and, one by one, in intervals of I'm not sure how long, put their noble parts inside my body. Professor Cevallos taught us to refer to it in that way, because according to him, it is man's most noble organ. I think there's nothing noble about it, because when they finally left me alone, tossed in a corner, trying to put my shorts back on, I felt a lot of pain in my stomach, as if they had ripped something inside of me, and as I turned on the light, I could see a thread of blood running slowly down one leg, until it reached my heel.

I got very scared and wanted to run out to the nurse's office so that she could give me a bandage or a cotton ball or a giant patch to stop the escape of my vital fluids, but I decided to stay there until I stopped hemorrhaging and the pain went away. Besides, I wasn't sure what I would say if someone asked me what had happened. Had I slipped when going down the stairs? No, no. I cleaned the blood from my body using my own shorts and then I wrapped them in a sheet of paper that I ripped from a magazine whose cover read *Life*.

I went immediately to the showers, being careful not to be seen. Inside I quickly got undressed and stood beneath the shower's stream so that the water would wash away any trace of blood that could be seen by the eyes of my bunk partner. Only dear God knows what would have happened if Juan Rodriguez had seen me, since this boy is one of the biggest gossips in our dorm. I washed my shorts with a bar of soap that I found lying on the tiles, blackened by dirt and water. I wrung my shorts out as hard as I could, until I drew the last drops of water from the cotton fibers. And, still damp, I put them on after I finished showering. I finished getting dressed, and my clothes became damp from my still-wet body. Shivering—whether from fear or from the cold, I don't know—I returned to the library so as to finish my homework. I was just walking in when I ran into Armando.

"Well, Witchy," he said, "what's wrong? Why are you trembling, and why are your clothes wet?"

"Nothing's wrong," I answered.

I sat down and continued reading my history book, on the same page where I had left it opened when those three big kids arrived.

"No," he said, "someone *did* something to you and you don't want to tell me. What happened? Did the guys throw you in cold water? Did they hit you?"

After Marcelo finished putting in and taking out his thing from me, he had clearly advised me: "You better not tell anyone about this, because we are going to beat the living shit out of you if you do." For that reason I stayed quiet during my friend's interrogation.

"No one did anything to me," I repeated to him. But he didn't believe me and instead hounded me with more questions. Finally, feeling cornered by the serious look in his eyes that demanded to know the truth, I told him everything. Totally. After everything they had already done to me, what did it matter if they beat me up or not?

When he saw me trembling and crying, he hugged me tightly and wiped away the tears that ran down my face.

"Fuckers! Sons of bitches! Bastards! But don't worry, Witchy, from now on I'll take care of you; I'll protect you. And I feel sorry for any guy who tries to touch you or treat you like that again, because now he'll have to answer to *me*. Come on, let's go out to the patio so your clothes will dry."

Putting his arm around my back, he escorted me out. We arrived downstairs where the three boys who had used me "for their own pleasure," as Armando had said, were in a corner talking as if nothing had happened.

"Go into the game room," he said. "I'll be right back for you."

He strode toward the three boys. I hadn't yet gotten to the door when I heard Marcelo's voice scream out:

"Don't get involved with this, it's none of your business!"

"I'm just warning you," Armando shouted. "If you or the other two do something to this poor kid again, I'll come and beat the crap out of you." And he added: "Because you three deserve nothing more than to have the crap beaten out of you!"

Once this exchange was over, he began walking toward the game room where I awaited him, but he hadn't even taken five steps when Genaro, the biggest of the three, yanked him by the shirt and he fell to the ground. Immediately, the other two joined him and they began to kick him mercilessly, until Señor Dominguez came and separated them.

"Okay, let's hear it. Why are you fighting?"

"We hit him because he cursed at us," said one of them.

"Is that true, Armando?"

"Yes, it's true; but I cursed at them because they cursed me first."

"Well," he said, "so that you'll learn to stop cursing and not use that sort of language, go and run one hundred and fifty laps around the yard and make sure you don't lose count, because I'll make you run another hundred and fifty."

In pain and almost out of breath, Armando completed his punishment. I watched him silently from the sidelines. At the end of each lap, he looked at me, just lowering his face a little, as if he was trying to tell me not to say anything more.

Armando's heroism inspired in me great admiration and respect. Since that day in the library, he has taken good care of me. He shares everything with me daily, and if I'm hungry, he gives me almost all his food. Sometimes he doesn't even get to eat a piece of his bread, just to make certain I eat well.

Every time I'm near him, when he holds me close to his body, I feel protected and well taken care of. By his side, I don't feel the time pass as slowly in this place where everything has changed, absolutely everything. For now the windows have been secured with thick iron bars and they've placed as many as three padlocks on each door. Why? Because two days after the onset of springtime, seven of the boys escaped while the rest of us slept.

No one heard anything because they made little noise, even when they broke the glass window from the tower which faced the garden next to the church, to get past the night watchman. They were caught on the mountain the following day, hopelessly lost and clueless about which road to take. The order given by the State Governor, to protect with maximum security all doors and windows, was followed to the letter of the law. If anyone had any prior knowledge of the escape, they said nothing. We were all afraid to say a word, as no one knew what might happen if one of us betrayed them. You could smell the fear from the moment they were brought back to school, because they had been beaten very badly. Their eyes were swollen and their uniforms were reduced to tatters. One of them returned bare-footed and one of his legs appeared to be broken. It was supported by two wooden boards tied together by a length of cord. They put all seven in confinement for two weeks and gave them only stale bread and a pot of cold coffee. They were merciless with the escapees and let no one defend them or plead on their behalf.

When they were finally taken out of there, they were thin and yellow and not one of them could stand without assistance. Santiago Diaz got typhoid fever because he was bitten by a black rat while in the cold darkness of the cell. He died a few days later from complications of an infection in his left leg, which had developed gangrene.

"Rabies die along with the dog!" proclaimed the director, loud enough so that we all heard as we returned from burying him at the west end of the castle.

"I hope this will be a lesson to all of you, because, starting today, there will be no more kindness at Los Molinos."

From that moment on, he prohibited us from listening to the radio and moved the television to his house, letting us know that he would be putting it in his son Tito's room. He also forbade anyone from going to town since, according to him, we had no business going there at all. Can you believe that he didn't even let Oscar, Miguelito, or myself go and finish our catechism classes so that we could do our First Communion? Nor were we allowed to go out to accept the Day of the Dead Offering, nor to celebrate Christmas Day as we had the years before.

I'm now thirteen years old, and because I'm older, I'm no longer as dumb and naive as I used to be. Now, I don't let the big boys come and tell me: "Come on, Witchy, let's go and do what I really like to do." No, those days are over. I've changed. I only go with them to the library or any other dark corner of the school when they give me something or if they bring me food, which daily becomes scarcer. Only that way will I let them do what they want to, and if they don't want to give me anything, I stay with Armando and contemplate the afternoons through the long bars. And if my buddy is busy and I can't see him, then I go and ask Leonora if she wouldn't like me to help her with any of the housework. And since I know she never says no, you'll find me there polishing the turquoise blue floors and washing her three children's clothes, and, once in a while, her panties and her husband's underwear. And as I wash and wash, I spend the time singing "La Canción del Preso":

If my death were due to you
With your heart's scorn,
If your arms cause my death,
There will be no prisoner happier than I…

I like to go to her house, because—besides its being very warm in there—she feeds me the same food she prepares for her own family, and when I can, I hide some of that same food in my clothes for my friend Armando. My dear and faithful Armando, with eyes the color of hope and a large, light-skinned body.

Guardian of my fears, vault of my dreams, and source of these, my first emotions. Next to him and with the passing of the months, I have learned to operate looms, to fabricate shoes, to make pants, and to know the world even more, through the pages of books.

Since that afternoon, when they punished Armando because of me, I've also shed my loneliness and the oppressive burden of monotony and routine. And when we lay our faces against the glass windows, I dream that someday we will be very far away from here, from this damn reform school where we're locked in....

Dallas, Summer 1986

Raúl Coronado Jr.

On weekends during the muggy, sweaty summer of 1986, I'd wait for my sisters y mami to leave the house. The car was barely out of the driveway before I'd call Rafael. In our year of sex, we rarely talked about it. We pretended nothing was going to happen. Funny—we both knew what we wanted, but never said a word about it. Only our actions would tell.

For me, sex was inseparable from my fear of being found out. The more I wanted it, the more I got it, the more I feared that people would read me and see what I had done the weekend before in the alleys, on the school rooftop, in my own house.

Walks down hallways in junior high became anxiety-ridden; I became paranoid of the way I walked. Could people tell that I had gotten fucked? Had my body begun to transform into something so queer that I could be ID'd at a glance? I spent hours in the shower, scrubbing those sex smells off of my teenage body, terrified that someone would smell me out.

As soon as Rafael told me he'd be over, I ran to my room, closed the windows, pulled the curtains, locked the doors, and turned up the radio. I shut off my room from the rest of the house and from the window-unit air conditioner. Within seconds, I could feel the August humidity begin to hang heavy in the room. My blood pumped faster, my heart started racing. I knew no one was home, but I was desperate to make sure nothing messed up our time together.

I'd pull out the Othello game board and put on the Bangles. I'd crank it up to drown out the rest of the world. Lying on the bed, we'd start playing, pretending we were interested in the game. After five minutes, the action would start.

The movements were barely detectable. You'd take off your shoes. You were always so in control. You were a man, a real fourteen-year-old man with a body that everyone noticed had grown a little faster than average. Your voice was deep, your body powerful, your attitude tough and confident. Your hurried walk in the humid heat had concocted a pungent scent. I could smell you. And you'd be mine for the next hour. Next to me, I'd let you take me, do what you wanted to me, as long as I could claim you. As long as I could feel you.

Move by move, we got closer. First, our hands started to brush up against each other. Our feet got closer.

The heat built up in that air-tight room. Sweat collected on my brow, our clothes became drenched, the heat intensified, and I no longer knew if it was because I wanted you so desperately or because of the residues of the dying Saturday afternoon heat. Knowing that any spoken word would betray your maleness, your straightness, you preferred to communicate by gestures. I knew better than to say what I wanted you to do. So I bit my lip, sweat hanging off my brow, as my hand came to rest near your thigh. In the background, I could hear the Bangles singing, "It's just another Manic Monday."

The smells in the room became my incense. Your musky scent, the salty stench of sweat. I cherish these smells. I refused to wash my sheets. Your odor infused them. I was desperate to keep any memory of you. A piece of clothing, your Boy Scout shirt that I borrowed and never returned, your maroon briefs—the first colored briefs I ever saw—the dirty pair of socks you left one time: I'd keep them all. Years later, I'd yearn for those smells.

I desired your strength. I wanted you to control me, dominate me, overpower me. In doing that, I'd get into you, below the layers of your arrogance, of your power to humiliate. For that one moment, I'd feel your softness, see your vulnerability, give you pleasure. But you'd always remind me that you were a man. You refused to kiss me, whispered "Faggot" in my ear when we were with the guys. And it worked. I was always afraid of you. I wanted you, but I was terrified to make the first move. But that was all I needed: a hint. Only give the sign, Rafael, and I would be healed.

Your damp athletic sock comes to rest lightly on mine. You rub your foot across my ankle; your fingers rest near my forearm. You stroke, grab your crotch, rough, not gentle at all, and you bring my hand toward it. The world speeds up.

We peel our clothes off. And I let you take control. I'm still awkward with these parts of my body. And it thrills me to know that you can guide me through it, teach me the uses of my body. You start and I feel like I'm being torn apart, and I whimper, ask for you to stop. But you coax me, you whisper in my ear, and your sweet moist breath down my neck is enough to convince me that this is right for me.

An hour later, we leave the place, steaming.

This was our ritual for an entire year. Once a week I could count on having you. On you teaching me about my body, teaching me the joys of Vaseline, becoming familiar with the pain and pleasures that sprang from your fingers' tracing my inner thighs.

I'd learn to share you with the stories you'd tell me about all the girls you had had that week: with your cousin in the deserts of West Texas, with a girl in the bushes by the bus stop, at your friend's house party. You probably lied to me, I told myself, to make yourself feel better for having sex with a guy. I'd still get jealous, and you knew it. But you'd proceed anyway and tell me the details of sex with girls. In the end, however, I'd have you, hold you, claim you. You may have had your girlfriends, but how many of them had you been with for a year?

In the back of my mind, I wondered what could've happened if you had publicly claimed our relationship. In the back of my mind, I imagined you bragging about fucking me, like you bragged about the girls.

"You're my ho'," you told me once. You could have me or any girl whenever you wanted. That was true, I was at your mercy. I was constantly begging for sex, so you told me—an insatiable desire to be close to men. A desire that has not diminished in the least over the past twelve years. You teased me, flirted with me. During our countless phone conversations, you'd inevitably allude to it. Make me beg for it. And I did. You could have anyone, you convinced me. I could have only you, I told myself.

You teased me, telling me that you'd have to start charging me 'cuz I wanted it so bad. You didn't expect it, but I told you to go to hell. That I had had enough of you. That sex with you was not worth the hell you put me through.

But a week later, it was you who came back to me. It was you who could not stay away.

Once, after one of our sweat-drenched summer sessions, as I put on my dirty socks, I watched you get dressed. I saw you leave me. Sitting at the edge of the bed naked except for the socks, I stared beyond you; I wondered where this would lead. When we would be able to be together.

I dreamt a beautiful dream of us leaving Oak Cliff, of moving somewhere together and living as man and wife. You would work in construction like the men in your family, and I'd study like I always had. But that dream quickly came to an end. You turned around and caught me dreaming.

And you changed. The Rafael I had for that hour each week would inevitably change, become hostile, see me as that which you despised in yourself.

"Raúl, are you gay?" you asked me, seeming to condemn me without needing an answer.

I wasn't prepared, Rafael, didn't you see? I didn't know what to say. You already had too much power over my life, and I could not give you any more. On weekends, with our friends, I'd become the object of derision: the one who studied too much, the one who didn't know how to play football, the one who didn't sniff talleewa, the sensitive mama's boy; I was the nerd of the group. I'd stare at you as you fell in with the guys, flinching each time your flared tongue spat out an attack. I'd wait for the day that you'd use the final weapon against me, wait until you sold me out, wait until you told the world the truth about me—that I was a joto, a faggot, a maricon, that I got screwed, and not only once, and even loved it. I held back, Rafael. I had to. I became afraid that this too would become your weapon. I knew I was queer, Rafael. I knew that I cherished your smell after playing football, that I loved the way you gently inflicted pain and pleasure on my body, that I could pleasure you as well. So I couldn't give you that ammunition. I loved you so much, I thought, but I just couldn't give in to the possibility of your using it against me. So I lied to you: I told you I wasn't. It came out more as a question than an affirmation. In that long year we were together, Rafael, this is as close as we got to talking about what we did.

"Are you gay, Raúl?"

But I wasn't willing to let go of the moment, to let it pass. I took a chance, and I asked you, whispered it, I think, "No, are you?"

I thought you hadn't heard me. You pulled on your tank top, turned around, and as you started to walk out, I think I heard you murmur: "No, I'm not."

Daddycakes

Randy Pesqueira

My father was in a motorcycle club in the early fifties. Before Marlon Brando's *Wild One* created the fast and crazy image of leather jackets and pissing contests. My dad was a Rambler, my mother a Ramblerette, and they built a clubhouse of their own—my dad, some uncles, and other men I would never meet. A bunch of teenage Mexican guys in a small town in Central California playing out the American game. But the Ramblers looked sharp, dark brown motorcycle shirts, brown leather jackets: sharp. I listened to my dad's stories as I grew up, all about the parties they had, and the runs in which everyone cruised up and down the state.

Dad's motorcycle comes to mind on a fast ride; I can feel it whenever I take off on a plane. I can feel the wind in my hair, the huge engine between my legs, and the thrill of being nestled into my father's massive frame. I was in heaven on that bike. Four or five years old, wearing darling little Disney sunglasses, looking ever so cool, and as my father whooshed into gear I lost my breath, and out popped one of the dark lenses, then the other, and into the wind went my cool look. I tried to tell my dad but he couldn't hear me until we came to a stop sign. I was crying about my glasses as I held the plastic frames in my hand. There is a look in my dad's eyes; I've seen it over the years. I remember seeing it for one of the first times that morning, the look that says he will do anything to make me feel better, to stop the crying, a *no llores, mijo* soft-faced look that means he will drive back and we will try to find the dark lenses to the plastic sunglasses, and so back we go —and he looks and looks, we find one then the other, one is thoroughly scratched. He fixes them for me, the first in a long history of things he would fix, we get going, start up; he puts them back on me and I feel cool again.

My father started working when he was twelve years old, or so the story goes. I think every Chicano kid's father from my generation started working when they were twelve, sometimes ten. It's almost as if they all reached puberty when they were eight, because many of them were married and had two kids by the time they were sixteen. Life was short. The San Joaquin Valley was homebase to my parents. After touring the state following the crops, setting up tents to live in and working long, long hard days, their families settled down. They were second or third generation Mexican-Hyphen-Americans, true bilinguals; they knew Spanish but were beaten by schoolteachers for speaking it. It was something they wouldn't teach us. Dad married Mom when he was twenty. She was sixteen. Within two years they'd have two girls. I came later, probably unplanned. Roy and Lola and the two darling girls moved to Orange County right before I was born, leaving behind the dusty hot summers and foggy winters to become the only Mexican family on the block in the lovely racist city of Santa Ana. It was a time in Orange County when Mexicans were allowed at the public pools one day only: the day before they cleaned it. It was still common to see signs that read: "No Dogs or Mexicans Allowed." Chicanismo was in its formative stages then. But our parents were proud to be Americans, remembering the thirties, when having brown skin was reason enough to send you to Mexico, whether you were born there or not.

Second Street in downtown Santa Ana: it's not even there now, but my first remembrance revolves around a bottle of green Prell shampoo. I am in the bathtub with my dad and he is sitting behind me very much like on the motorcycle ride. He is washing my hair and I can smell the strong fresh scent and I can feel the strong hands on my head and I am the most protected boy in the world. My Daddy loves me. I was always sick and they needed to yank my tonsils by the time I was three. I would get delirious fevers and had to be dipped into ice-cold water. There was no fresh scent of Prell shampoo during those baths, but I would be rocked to sleep in my dad's arms. I believe it was at that time that I began to grow an appreciation for big strong masculine arms. It was right after this that I ended up in the hospital for the tonsil yanking. It scarred my memories. Images of big ugly nurses, the feeling of being abandoned, and the very painful reality of having a thermometer shoved up my then-tiny ass. I was told to be a big boy, not to cry. But everything hurt so much.

Be a big boy. The baths with my father ended. He sold the motorcycle and pretty soon all I knew of my father surrounded the lunch box that he took to work. It was black, with a curved top. He worked second shift at the Anaconda plant in Orange. I remember my mom fixing us dinner and then packing up his lunch box so we could take it to him. I would sit in the back of the blue-green Chevy station wagon holding his lunch box. My mom and I would wait for him to come out for his break; I believe he got a whole twenty minutes. He'd swallow down the big burritos wrapped in aluminum foil, guzzle a bottle of Coca-Cola, and then off he would go. Work was his life; often there were weekend jobs. But then there were the parties.

We had this massive backyard, half the size of a football field, it seemed. Whenever there was an occasion for a party, we had it. You could make your own beer then, and my dad's was the best. On big holidays, all the *compadres*, *comadres*, and my wonderful *tias* would come down and party. Songs by José Alfredo Jimenez and Cuco Sanchez, Lola Beltran, Patsy Cline, and later Edye Gorme floated through my head. The homemade margaritas and the chicken and mole and always turkey on Thanksgiving. As the evenings wore on, the crying would begin. All it took was the right combination of alcohol and sad song and everyone would be hugging each other. Sometimes there'd be a fight. My dad, a normally quiet man, would start arguing when drunk. He was always tough, a bit of argument in English and in Spanish, and if anyone pissed him off too much he was known to throw some *chingasos.* I think the most I ever did was kick someone with my Beatles boots.

I always wondered what he thought of his sissy son. And I *was* a sissy. Once my *Nino* Joe wanted me to play baseball like his two sons. I refused. I did go to the baseball diamond as told, but I ended up on the swings. No "hey batter batter" for me; that ball was going too fast. I mean, if they played a sort of softball underhanded pitch kind of thing, it might have been different. My dad never said anything, a kind of silent understanding. I liked baggy sweaters, the kind that hung off one shoulder. I would sit for hours and watch my older sisters put on their makeup, and I could dance the twist with the best of them. But it was OK for men to dance, because in our house Dad always danced with Mom.

As a teen queen I was the first to wear bellbottoms to my junior high school—navy-blue Nuvo flares from Levi's at the Army & Navy. I believe my dad drove me to the store to get them. Pretty smooth. And then platform shoes came out and I just didn't have platform shoes, I had huge clog types with thick cork soles. I'd wear them with my best plaid polyester pants, and I'd wear them to family reunions in the San Joaquin Valley. My dad would smile and call me crazy. Years later when I dyed my hair the most brilliant teal green to match a certain sweater, I think he was taken aback. All he asked was how was I going to get a job looking like that. He didn't know I was already working for the gay and lesbian center.

My respect for my father only grew. I started doing AIDS work in 1983. Within a couple of years, my mother was one of my best volunteers and soon after that, so was my dad. They worked with a young Mexican couple; a husband contracted AIDS from a transfusion in Mexico, had infected his wife, and she was pregnant. He ended up being my dad's new *compadre,* eighties style. They took this couple in like anyone else, showering them with healing love and genuine care. The *compadre* died a couple of years later, she soon after that; she and Dad were still close. Their child, who is HIV negative, was adopted by my cousins. And so it goes on.

Daddycakes is what I can call him now, Pops, Daddy, any endearing term. He moves slower, but he still has those strong arms. He has never shown anything but respect for my gay friends, or my now ex-husband. He still fixes things for me, works on my long and lovely T-Bird; he works hard eight hours a day and sometimes Saturday. He has helped to raise five grandchildren and now has three great-grandchildren who will forever know him as *Tata.*

AIDS work taught us the term *unconditional love.* I didn't have to be taught what it was; I was familiar with the model before the term became a catchword. From the time Dad first fixed my broken sunglasses to his crying over the loss of his *compadre,* I don't know if I've ever thanked him enough.

The Lost City

Rodolfo Zamora

The Lost City wasn't really a city. It was the name given by school officials to a row of five small roach-infested apartments hidden by scrubby desert bushes and laurel trees that bloomed pink and white flowers. I lived in one of them, the one in the center, with Papa, my sisters Angelica and Maria, my brother Juan, Prima Irma who had recently arrived from Mexico, Tia Marcelina, Tio Abel, my eldest sister Licha, her husband, and her two daughters.

Mama was in Mexico taking care of Abuelito, who was dying of cancer. It was his request to have his eldest daughter there with him during his last days. Abuelito's health neither improved nor worsened, so she stayed for many months.

I remember the day Mama received a registered letter my sister read out loud to her. When Angelica finished reading it, Mama took it and reread the words, as if she was determined to find a hidden code that would negate her Papa's impending death.

It was a mystery to me to see how written words moved Mama to tears. Since I didn't understand the meaning of Abuelito's illness, I asked, "Ama, why are you crying?"

"*No es nada, mijo,*" she said, wiping her eyes, red from crying.

Later that day I heard the word *Mexico* many times from the lips of adults. Still crying, Mama packed her clothes that night in a blue vinyl suitcase with the help of her two comadres.

"I want to go to Mexico, too," I said.

"You can't go," she said. "You're going to school."

"*No, yo quiero ir,*" I said, and began digging inside a big cardboard box where we kept our clean clothes. I cried as I searched for my Sunday-best clothes to take with me. Mama didn't let me pack my things in her suitcase, but I didn't give up. I would go with her no matter what, I thought.

When I awoke the following morning she was gone. She had decided to take Juan with her. I believed she chose him because she loved him more than me. I felt abandoned by her, and I hadn't experienced anything like it before. Thereafter whenever I heard the train passing in the night, I imagined her return. I fantasized she was sleeping next to me on the floor, in the living room, where my two sisters and I slept.

We only traveled out of The Lost City to go to school or to Leon's Market, which were in the neighboring city of Mecca. I always made sure I was the first one in the back seat of my brother-in-law's orange Pinto. I even tolerated the weight of my nieces, who sat on my lap. Otherwise I had to get out, but I occasionally pinched them on our way there, and that felt good.

Aisle six was my favorite aisle, the stationery aisle, the reason I put up with the extra weight on my lap. There my love for pencil sharpeners began. I'd pass on Hostess Cakes and bubblegum any day for a pencil sharpener. I collected one a week in every available color. "What do you want another one for?" Papa would always say.

"It's not the same one. This one's yellow," I'd respond. Acquiring a sharpener depended on two things: Papa's mood, which was easier to work with when he had recently gotten paid, or if he was a little drunk. One time I got away with two, a green one and a red one, on the same day.

I liked to sharpen pencils more than playing with toy soldiers or marbles. I sharpened pencils even if they didn't need to be sharpened. It was like magic, the way a pencil disappeared. I imagined the plastic top where the spirals collected as a clean, empty house. I experienced a great satisfaction filling it up to the point where they were all crushing each other, especially with shavings that didn't break right away. Then I would go outside, remove the top, and release them out into the air. Emptying it out was like witnessing thousands of butterflies unfurl their wings and let the wind carry them to a new life. In my mind, our one-bedroom apartment was transformed into a big house with a room for each person. After this I'd wash the top with soapy water, making sure no pencil lead was visible. If it sparkled I smiled, convinced it was the most immaculate house on the planet.

A set of twelve pencils would be gone in a week's time. I sharpened at school during recess, blowing spirals out from the top of the slide, and at home all hours of the day, even while I watched Scooby Doo. I even dared to free them out the bus window one time, and got a bus citation.

I hid all twelve sharpeners under Papa's bed, including the repeated colors of red and blue, along with a small photograph of Mama inside a green, plastic index card holder I'd found in the stationery aisle. Mama's photograph, though cracked and brown like an aging leaf, still revealed a fresh, youthful smile that powerfully evoked the warmth of her presence and the scent of her nurturing embrace.

"Get your clothes ready," Papa said "we're going to Oxnard tomorrow."

"Is it farther than Mecca ?" I asked. He laughed when I asked him how many moons would follow me before we got there.

That night I didn't sharpen any pencils. I was going to a new place. I knew Papa expected me to wear the three-piece dark blue suit I wore only on the first day of school and on school picture day, along with the long-sleeve shirt with designs of little choo-choo trains on it. I would get to wear my shiny new shoes, which I hadn't worn because Papa had forbidden me to wear them.

Before going to bed that night Prima Irma said, "Oxnard is the most beautiful place, even more beautiful than Mexico. You'll get to eat the sweetest strawberries, the size of apples. And you'll get to see Abuelita, who loves you so much. She'll take good care of you."

I went to bed feeling loved by a woman I didn't know. The happiness I felt kept me awake for a long time. Although I hadn't met Abuelita, she appeared in a dream that night, as an old woman with gray hair, wearing a blue apron, calling me, holding a basket full of apple-sized strawberries.

For the first time, Papa didn't have to wake me. I was up before all of them, worried they'd forget to take me along. I made sure to apply Papa's *Tres Flores* brilliantine to give my hair extra shine, slathering on so much that I would've slid right out of Abuelita's arms had she tried to hug me.

"You look so *guapo,*" Irma said as we left The Lost City behind. "Abuelita is going to be so proud to have a *nieto* as handsome as you. And look at your shoes—you look like *un hijo de* Kennedy."

At that moment I realized I'd forgotten my sharpeners, but I didn't care. I was going to meet a woman who loved me.

Twenty minutes into our trip I was already seeing new things. There were so many markets—some bigger, some smaller than Leon's.

We were lost.

"I'm telling you that you're going the wrong way," Licha said to her husband.

"When's the last time *you* traveled out of The Lost City?" her husband said.

"You talk as if you designed the goddamn streets," said Licha, lowering her window.

"Do I have to remind you that it was me who worked in Oxnard last year, when you refused to come with me?" he said.

"I didn't refuse to go. I told you that I couldn't work bending over all day long picking strawberries. You know damn well I have back problems."

I noticed Papa was getting upset, because he was massaging his Adam's apple. Finally, he asked them to pull over. He said he wasn't going anywhere with them, that he'd rather walk back home. Everyone in the car remained silent as my brother-in-law turned around and headed back to The Lost City. I felt a tension in my throat that made me want to scream in frustration. But I couldn't utter a sound. Then Irma said to me, "*Que pena, te quedaste vestido y alborotado,*" reminding me I was dressed up with nowhere to go.

At first she was serious, but the more markets we passed, the funnier it became to all of them, including Papa, who tried not to laugh by biting his upper lip. When he finally couldn't hold it, they all exploded with laughter, and I began to cry. "I want to see Abuelita. I want strawberries."

"*Dicen que los hombres no deben llorar por una mujer...*" Irma sang the song I hated, making me cry even louder.

"Shut up!" I screamed.

"You shouldn't talk that way to an adult," said Licha.

"Papa, tell her to be quiet," I said, crying.

Then Papa did something I'd never forget: he took me in his arms, tenderly, the way I imagined Abuelita embracing me, and said in a calm voice that silenced my sobs, "Don't worry, Abuelita will always be in Oxnard waiting for you."

When we got back I ran into the apartment, grabbed my green box from under the bed, and locked myself in the bathroom. I placed Mama's photograph on top of a roll of toilet paper, and sat on the edge of the bathtub. Looking at Mama's photograph, I ignored the knocks on the door, and sharpened away till all twelve sharpeners were ready to burst with swirls.

My Lessons with Felipe

James Cañón

Felipe and his pimples came to live with us in April of 1963. He had as many pimples on his face as we had coffee beans on our farm. My father was his godfather, so when Felipe's parents got killed by mistake during a shooting in Fresno, he moved in with us. "He's had enough school already," my father said. "Besides, harvest season is just around the corner and we can use an extra hand on the farm." Felipe was seventeen years old and had just finished high school.

The idea of sharing my bedroom with Felipe came from my father, and the protest came from me.

"I don't want to share my bedroom with a stranger!"

"Felipe is not a stranger." My father replied. "Besides, there are no more rooms in the house."

"Put him with Pedro and Juan," I moaned, suggesting my younger brothers' room.

"You only think of yourself!" My father yelled. "I'm not going to squeeze three guys in one room so that you can be alone. Now, if being alone is what you want, I can make room for you in the attic," he added, and I knew that that wasn't an offer but a threat. The attic was filled with memories of Mamá. She had died three years before: the brown dress she loved to wear to mass on Sunday, the new white dress she was going to put on for the day of my first communion, her aprons, her hats, her shoes, and a long braid of her black hair that my father cut off after she died and had kept in a brown wooden box. But Mamá's goods were not alone; the attic was also full of mice, snakes, and God knew what else, so I decided to share the room without further protest.

A folding bed and a night table were placed next to mine; and in the corner, where I used to kneel down to say my prayers to my mother, an empty wooden trunk was now awaiting Felipe's belongings. Sitting on my bed, I thought how uncomfortable it was going to be to sleep in the same room with a stranger, to hear him snoring, to have to smell his farts; so I got up and pushed my bed all the way against the only window, and his bed all the way against the opposite wall—that way we'd be as far from each other as the square room allowed us to be. I sat on my bed again and couldn't help imagining the intruder picking his nose and scratching his butt; so I got up again and placed both my chest of drawers and his empty trunk between the beds. That would be the border, the line of demarcation between his space and mine; that way we wouldn't have to see each other if we didn't want to.

It was siesta time. I was lying on my bed when Felipe came into my room without knocking first. He stood up by the door with one bag in each hand, and a full smile on his pimpled face. He was taller than I was, and if my skin was the color of coffee and milk, Felipe had much more milk than coffee in his. His uncombed black hair looked greasy, but his clothes were clean and pressed.

"Hi, David. I'm Felipe, remember me?" He asked in a deep, throaty voice. I looked at him from head to toe and from toe to head, then I shook my head.

"Come on, David. Try harder. We all used to play hide and seek when we were kids," he added with a little frustration in his hoarse voice. I shook my head again.

"Come on," he cried like a spoiled baby while putting his bags down on the wooden floor. "I'll give you another clue: Once, you and I hid in an empty coffee sack. All the kids passed by us yelling our names, not knowing we were inside the sack." He burst into laughter. "Haha-haha-haha-haha...." And that's when I remembered who he was. His short sequences of "hahas" were unforgettable; besides, my brothers and I made fun of his laughter long after he and his brothers stopped visiting us.

"They didn't find us," he continued. "And we ended up falling asleep inside the sack, haha-haha-haha-haha...." Three minutes hadn't gone by since his arrival and he was already annoying me.

"I bet you remember me now, right, David?" he asked confidently.

"No. I don't remember your ugly face," I lied out of anger, and then lay down on my stomach to avoid seeing him. Felipe ignored my childish reaction and started unpacking while singing to himself, "Lalalalá-lalá-lalá...." I covered my head with a pillow and tried to fall asleep, but his tune and the cracking noise he made walking back and forth over the wooden floor made it impossible.

"Boy, we're going to have fun together," he said. "You're going to have to show me around again. I want to pick fresh guavas and oranges, ummm.... I want to run up and down the hill, go swimming in the stream; there's a stream, isn't there? I want to check out wild birds' nests...." Felipe's list of things to do sounded endless. He kept on telling me about his plans, and I kept on ignoring him until I fell asleep.

I woke up to the sound of the bell calling all the *peones* back to the coffee fields. It must have been about two in the afternoon. The first thing I saw was Felipe lying down on his bed, with a book in his hands and a smile on his face. He had moved the boundaries I had created; my chest of drawers was now against the wall, and his trunk was in the corner where it had been placed first. Little piles of books were all over the room, and a framed picture of a young couple was hanging on the wall, right above his head.

"I like our bedroom better this way. Now I can see who I'm talking to. What do you think?" It took me a few seconds to get up from the bed, and a few more to answer:

"This is my bedroom and I want it the way I had it!" I yelled, and started pushing the chest back to where I had it.

"All right. I'll give you a hand."

"I can do it by myself." I tried to stop him.

"No way. Four hands are better than two." And he helped me put the two pieces of furniture back between the beds.

"Where do you want me to leave all my books?" he asked with concern.

"I don't care, as long as they are on your side of the room." And with that answer I left for work, convinced that I had proved my point of being the decision-maker in the room. From the long hall, I heard his "Lalalalá-lalá-lalá..." growing softer as I walked away.

Felipe was quickly given duties of his own. He had to get up at three in the morning and grind thirty pounds of boiled corn for the *arepas.* Then Rosario, the cook, and the maids kneaded the ground corn into dough, molded it by hand into the shape of medium-sized plates, and finally roasted about two hundred *arepas* over coal. At five in the morning, when the roosters started singing, Felipe had to help the maids serve breakfast to the almost one hundred *peones* that came from other towns to help during harvest time. Each one would stand in line for a bowl of eggs and some onion soup, a fresh-roasted *arepa,* and a cup of *café con leche.* Right after breakfast, Felipe and the *peones* went to the coffee plantations and began collecting red coffee beans in big baskets tied to their bodies.

Neither my two younger brothers, Pedro and Juan, nor I had ever gone to school. The closest one was in El Hatillo, a small village far away in the middle of the mountains.

"It's a three-hour walk," I said to my brothers. "By the time we get to school our feet are going to be sore."

"We can use Matea," Juan suggested, pointing at the old pack mule.

"That poor mule can't hold the three of us," Pedro said in disbelief. "Look at it. It can hardly carry its own bones."

"And even if it could, by the time we get there, each of us will have one of its bones up the ass," I added, thinking of how painful it would be to ride the scrawny mule twice a day, for two or three hours. On the other hand, my father didn't quite encourage us to go to school.

"School is for the stupid," he had said to us. "Look at me; I never went to school and I own this farm. I gave your mother everything she wanted, and you can't complain yourselves; you have never gone to work before filling up your *barrigas* with a full bowl of soup and a cup of *café con leche*," he added proudly.

My job on the farm was to weigh the coffee beans that each peón had collected. Since I was illiterate, I'd have Rosario, the cook, write the numbers down on a piece of paper. Rosario thought herself indispensable, for she was the only one who could read and write. She was in her early twenties: a fat cow, always eating, burping, and farting. I could tell by the authority in her voice and by the many privileges she had around the farm that she and my father were sleeping together. Rosario wasn't pretty—no woman my father slept with was anywhere near as pretty as my mother had been. However, some of Rosario's features, like her big green eyes under thick black eyebrows, though not nearly as radiant as Mamá's, somehow reminded me of hers. Rosario also loved to cook and clean, and there was nothing more convenient to my father than a young domestic woman who could read and write.

I began to see Felipe with different eyes after he gave me the first lesson.

"You have to learn to write and read. You must," he insisted over and over for a few days, but I showed no interest whatsoever.

"David, you can't always depend on Rosario. You need to learn how to do basic mathematical calculations, so that nobody takes advantage of you or your father." I don't know if it was the fear of being manipulated by Rosario, or the challenge of being the only one in my family who could read and write, or just the wish of being able to do my work by myself, without having to put up with Rosario's burps, farts, and attitude; I don't know what it was, but I decided to give it a chance.

The class began at six-thirty, right after dinner, in my side of the room. He started with the vowels, and in less than two hours, I found myself sounding out *a, e, i, o, u*. Later on, Felipe ended my first lesson with a gentle pat on the back of my head.

"You're a very smart guy," he said. "Go to sleep now, I'm going to read for a while." He blew out the candle that was on my night table and went to his side of the room. I closed my eyes and thought about Felipe. He had just spent a few hours teaching me letters patiently, ignoring my selfish behavior and all the mean things I had said to him. "Should I apologize?" I asked myself. "But, what could I say? Maybe I'll just start all over again and try to be his friend." I kept thinking of different ways to make it up to him, and decided to start by thanking him for giving me the first lesson. I opened my eyes; the light of the candle on his night table was still illuminating part of the room, and I heard him undressing. I knelt on my bed to see, over my chest of drawers, what he was doing. He was half-naked, looking under the pillow for his pajama trousers.

"What are you doing?" I asked, pretending not to know. He grabbed the pillow and quickly covered his crotch with it.

"You scared me, David. I thought you were sleeping."

"I just want to...I just wanted to thank you for teaching me those letters."

"That's nothing, really. This is only the beginning. In a few months you're going to be reading and writing just like I do. You'll see." He continued holding the pillow against his body, and I kept staring at the pillow without saying a word.

"Go to sleep, David. We have to get up early tomorrow." Then he blew out the candle and I heard him putting on his pajama bottoms in the darkness.

"Why did you cover yourself with the pillow?" I asked.

"There are some things that you can't see. You're only thirteen years old," he almost whispered.

"But...you and I...I mean, you and I have the same..." I stammered.

"Yeah, we have the same, but different."

"I don't understand. The same but different?"

"Well...yours is a boy's, mine is a man's."

"I still don't understand."

"David, mine is bigger and has hair."

"Really? Mine just started growing little hair too," I said proudly. "Let me see yours."

"No way. Go to sleep."

"Come on, Felipe. Let me see it...come on." He didn't say anything else, so I pulled the bed clothes over my head and tried to imagine his man's penis, but nothing materialized. I then tried to fall asleep, and my last thought was that I had seen him half-naked and heard him undress, and that thought stayed with me even in my sleep that night.

The next morning I convinced my father to let Felipe be my helper at work.

"Felipe knows how to write and read, he knows the numbers, he knows everything."

"Is there any problem with Rosario?" he asked, intrigued by my unexpected request.

"No, Papá, but I think she likes the kitchen better."

"Of course she likes the kitchen better, she's a woman. The kitchen is the place where women belong."

Felipe was surely bright. He quickly learned his new duties, and he even helped me do my work so that the *peones* wouldn't waste any time. The day went by so much faster and we had fun working together.

"Rosario has all her farts confused," Felipe said mockingly. "They don't know whether to come out through her ass or through her mouth. Haha-haha-haha-haha...." I laughed too. He also gave funny nicknames to almost every *peón* who brought coffee to be weighed.

"The 'Pig Man' is coming," he whispered in my ear. I looked at the short, fat peón and burst out laughing. But we also talked about serious subjects, like our dead mothers.

"I say prayers to my mother every day," Felipe confessed to me.

"I say prayers to mine every day too." I was happy to have found one more thing in common with him.

"If you could have your mother back for one minute, what would you tell her?" he asked me. I thought about it for a few seconds. "I would just say, 'Mamá, I love you; Mamá, I love you...' until the minute was over," I said, remembering the night when she was dying in her room, and my father didn't let me go inside to say the last I-love-you, for he thought it would be too painful.

"What would you tell yours?" I asked, intrigued.

"I would tell her that I miss her so much, but that she can rest in peace now, because I have found another home and I'm happy."

At this point teardrops peeped out from our eyes, so we changed the topic. We talked about his two brothers and my two brothers, his life in Fresno, and my life on the farm; we made plans to go hunting rabbits and to see the waterfall; we began to be friends.

My second lesson also took place in our bedroom. Only by this time I had already moved the two pieces of furniture back against the wall, so that Felipe and I could see each other from our beds. This time we studied the alphabet, and even though I tried very hard I couldn't memorize the thirty letters. Felipe wasn't, however, the kind of person who gave up without trying a variety of tactics. He drew the letters in different colors; he looked for names of animals, flowers, fruits, and vegetables to help me relate easily to each letter; but I still couldn't recite the alphabet.

"What am I going to do?" he asked himself aloud. Then he stared pensively at the candle on my night table. "I know," he finally said. "If you memorize the whole alphabet by tomorrow night...I'll show you my penis." Then he blew out both candles, and I heard again the sound of his clothes falling to the floor. I waited a few more minutes until he started snoring, and then I went out to the patio and spent the whole night memorizing the thirty letters of the alphabet by moonlight, and imagining his penis being unveiled before my eyes.

The next day, right after breakfast, I recited the whole alphabet to Felipe without missing a single letter.

"I'm impressed. You memorized thirty letters overnight!" He seemed pleased with my progress.

"So...when am I going to see...what you promised?" I asked immediately.

"This evening, after dinner. Just wait for me by the stream, where the guava tree is."

I couldn't concentrate on my work that day: "What if his penis has pimples like his face?" I asked myself. "If that's the case I'm going to ask him to let me see his butt. It's kind of flat but I'm sure it's smooth." I also tried to picture the encounter. The sound of the water coming down the stream; Felipe coming down the hill singing his Lalalalá-lalá-lalá; the cool breeze; Felipe all naked, with just a pillow covering his penis; the scent of fresh guavas in the air; Felipe's pillow growing smaller and smaller as he gets closer to me.

The tortuous wait made it a very long day. I even lost my appetite for white rice and red beans—Rosario's every-night menu. I sat at the wooden table in the kitchen, across from Felipe, and my heart pounded. "How can he be eating," I thought, "chatting with my father, laughing with my brothers when something extraordinary is just about to happen? How?!"

"I'm sorry. I'm not hungry. I ate too much fruit this afternoon." I excused myself and went to the stream to wait for him.

Lying down on the grass, I closed my eyes and tried to relax. My heart pounded again, or maybe it hadn't stopped pounding all day. I couldn't feel the cool breeze or hear the water, and I certainly didn't smell the guavas. I can't even tell how long I waited for him before I heard his tune from a distance. I opened my eyes but remained in the same position; maybe this way he wouldn't notice how excited I was. "Lalalalá-lalá-lalá..." and my body started shaking, "Lalalalá-lalá-lalá..." and my mouth felt so dry, "Lalalalá-lalá-lalá...."

"It's beautiful down here," he finally said, standing next to me.

"Yes...very beautiful...down here," I agreed, with my eyes set on the sky.

"Well, are you ready?" He asked almost indifferently, as if he were just going to show me his big toe. I got up and stood in front of him, my hands closed so that he wouldn't see them shaking.

"Yes. I'm ready." He unbuttoned his brown pants and pulled them down to his knees, and I saw the bulk through his white briefs.

"Do you really want to see it?" he asked again.

"Yes. Yes, I really want to," I almost begged him. Then he pulled his underwear down and his penis swung from side to side; so did my eyes following it from left to right and from right to left until it stopped in the middle. It was beautiful. Much bigger and thicker than mine, and it had no pimples whatsoever. Wrinkled skin covered what I guessed was its big head, and I think I saw black short hair surrounding it.

"There it is," Felipe said, and then he added proudly: "Pretty big, isn't it?" I didn't say anything. I kept staring at it without blinking. I don't think I even breathed during the few seconds he left it out. He pulled up his white briefs, then his pants, buttoned up, and left singing his tune. I lay down on the grass again, under the guava tree, and masturbated thinking about Felipe, his beautiful smile, his harsh voice, his big hands, his penis. Suddenly, the pimples on his face didn't matter anymore.

The following day at work, we didn't mention anything, but I noticed that Felipe now had more important things to confide in me. He told me about Patricia, his girlfriend in Fresno. "She promised to wait for me until I go back," he said arrogantly. He also told me about the boarding school he went to, and he laughed when he recounted how all the boys used to make fun of him in the showers because his penis was too big. He got sad when he remembered Camilo, his roommate. "He was a great guy from Ibagué, not too tall but very handsome, like you. One night I woke up and found him all naked in my bed, right next to me; he said he was cold. I embraced him and warmed up his smooth body by rubbing my hands all over him. After that night, we slept naked in the same bed every night until we graduated.... I never saw him again, but sometimes, when the nights get windy and cold, I miss his little body next to mine." I was glad that Felipe had trusted me with the secrets of his heart, but at the same time I was jealous of Patricia and Camilo. I wanted to be one of Felipe's secrets; maybe that way I too would live inside of him.

My third lesson with Felipe was on the numbers. Uno, dos, tres, cuatro, and so on. To make it easier for both of us, Felipe had made a writing-board of a thin slab of wood he found in the attic. He painted it white, and we used pieces of charcoal to write on it. He drew the numbers from zero to nine, and pronounced them one by one while I repeated after him. Then he made new numbers by combining two of the single numbers; really easy, but I pretended to be confused so that he would spend more time with me, giving me all his attention.

"For tomorrow I want you to memorize the numbers from one to fifty. I know you can do it."

"That sounds like too many numbers, Felipe. Is there...any kind of reward for me to learn all of them," I asked with my head down, looking at the floor.

"Haha-haha..." he laughed timidly. "I don't know... I guess I'll let you see my penis again."

"But I saw it already," I protested. "I mean, I don't mean to be disrespectful, but seeing it one more time will only make me memorize half the numbers." I was determined to negotiate an even better reward this time. Felipe seemed confused for a few seconds, but then regained control of the situation.

"Learn as many numbers as you can," he said. "I promise you won't be disappointed with the reward."

I liked Felipe's lessons. I never thought learning letters and numbers could be this exciting. I wondered if that was the same way teachers taught in the school of El Hatillo; but José, the cowboy, had attended one year of elementary school, and he told me about this witchy-looking teacher with thick glasses, who used to break rulers on children's hands for not learning quickly enough. I was lucky. My teacher had pimples on his face but he was kind and patient, and he had a beautiful penis that was bigger than mine.

The next morning I recited the numbers from one to ninety-four, and then Felipe stopped me: "Boy...you seem to be learning fast. See me this evening. Same place, same time." And we didn't talk about it for the rest of the day.

I ate my rice-and-beans dinner as fast as I could, hoping Felipe would do the same; but he started talking to my father about the plans he had for his future.

"You know, *Padrino,*" He began. "I think I want to be a doctor...." Then he paused, waiting for my father's reaction.

"We don't need doctors around here," My father stated. "We have witches and *curanderos.* We don't even need medications because for each disease there is, we have a plant that cures it."

"It's not the same, *Padrino.* If a real doctor had treated my *madrina's* illness she wouldn't be dead now." He used his manly hands to make his argument more credible, but my father was stubborn and wouldn't give in.

They were still discussing the matter when I left the house. On my way to the stream I fantasized about the reward he had promised. "Maybe he'll show me his butt this time," I mused. "Maybe he'll let me play with his penis the way I play with mine. What if he asks me what I want for my reward? Well, in that case I'll suggest that we both lie down naked on the grass, and that he rub his hands all over my body, and that he embrace me the way he used to embrace Camilo."

There was still daylight when he showed up. He had combed his black hair, and he had the biggest, most radiant smile on his face.

"It's beautiful down here," he said. I noticed he was tense.

"Yes. Very beautiful." I too decided to go with the same line that had worked so well the first time. He looked up at the horizon for a few seconds, and then, without looking at me, he took off all his clothes.

"I want to test you one more time," he said when he was completely naked. "I want you to count all the moles on my body." Although lean, his body seemed muscular and well defined, and his skin appeared smooth and hairless.

"Where should I start?" I asked right away, thinking there was no time to waste. He didn't answer but offered his right hand. I began to count the moles aloud without delay, "Uno, dos, tres..." making sure not to skip even one, "nueve, diez, once..." traveling with my eyes from one arm to another, "veintidos, veintitres..." exploring behind his ears, across his back, "treinta y seis, treinta y siete..." around his buttocks, between his legs, "cincuenta y cinco, cincuenta y seis..." feeling on my sweaty skin the warmth of his body, the heat of mine, "setenta y uno, setenta y dos..." striving to ignore the rise of his penis, enjoying the growth of mine, "setenta y nueve, ochenta..." There was no part of his body I didn't check for moles to count, and when I finished, I added once again the moles that I had already counted, until the moonlight disappeared behind dark clouds and we heard the first thunder in the sky.

"I never realized I had that many moles on my body," Felipe said while collecting his clothes from the grass.

"I never realized I knew that many numbers," I replied, my eyes still set on his naked body. He knew I had cheated, and if he didn't stop me it was because he, too, had taken pleasure from the reward he had invented.

"Addition and subtraction is all about kisses," Felipe told me during my first mathematics lesson by the stream, and I knew it was going to be a very intense subject.

"Now, lie down on your back, close your eyes, and relax your body," he ordered. "To add means to sum, aggregate, to make it more, and the opposite of it is to subtract, which means to take away." He defined each term with such precision, but he knew I wouldn't fully understand the meaning of his words unless I had one of his creative representations. He pressed his lips against mine for less than a second.

"That was a kiss," he said.

"Was it really?" I asked in disbelief with my eyes still closed. "I didn't feel anything."

"There are many kinds of kisses."

"What kind was that one?"

"Doesn't matter. We're talking mathematics here." He got defensive. Then he gave me my first real kiss. His lips covered mine and pulled them gently into his mouth. His wet tongue rushed in and out of my mouth twice, maybe three times, and then stayed in there for not many seconds, exploring it. My tongue joined his and they both played inside his warm mouth. We did it all over again for a few times, and I thrust my fingers deep into the ground to avoid the temptation of touching my erect penis…or his.

"That was another kind of kiss," he stated, pleased with himself, and I didn't have anything to say. "So one kiss plus another kiss makes two kisses…," he continued. "Now, let me ask you, if I gave you another kiss, how many kisses would you have in your mouth?"

"Give me the kiss and I'll tell you."

"Haha-haha-haha-haha…." Then he kissed me one more time, and then another, and another until I lost count.

"How many kisses do you have now?" Felipe finally asked.

"Not enough," I answered, and we continued adding kisses to my mouth and subtracting them from his until dawn.

I never knew what kind of reward Felipe had for me to learn to multiply and divide, because one cold night in November he didn't come to meet me by the stream. I sat naked under the guava tree and waited hours to hear his "Lalalalá-lalá-lalá..." from a distance, but he never appeared. Later that night I found under my pillow a note that Felipe had written to me.

My very dear friend David,

I must say good-bye. My grandparents have decided that I should begin my college education, and so I'm leaving for Ibagué where there is a university. I was very pleased to meet the boy who didn't know the vowels, nor to kiss; but I'm delighted to leave a man who can write, read, and love. If you ever feel unloved, think of me.

Felipe

I folded the letter in four and put it in my chest of drawers. Then I lay down on my bed, holding his pillow tight against my chest. I looked through the window, and with tears in my eyes I started counting the stars in the sky as if they were moles on his body.

Delirium

News of Your Country

Roger Schira

He had not thought of Luquillo in many years and it was only because he was on this deserted beach that he was thinking of it now. Small pear-shaped leaves covered the sand and rose up into the golden autumn air when the wind hit them. They charged left and then right as if searching for some object to surround and subdue. They were like malevolent schools of fish angry at being trapped on land, eager to bite. He watched the leaves throw themselves up into the air, the coarse, dry sound of their bodies unpleasant. They came toward him in small, fervent whirlwind formations and beat against his trouser legs, and then a large leaf, from an elm or an oak tree, rose up and landed on his cheek, the wind pressing it hard against his skin so that it felt like a small hand there, insistent and taloned. He pushed it off and stood there a moment and looked out at the ocean, the wind dying down, the leaves exhausted and defeated at his feet.

That night he stood before the mirror in his bedroom and removed his clothing. He looked at his body carefully, touching his leg, smoothing a patch of graying hair on his chest, arching his neck slightly. He touched his penis with one hand, turning it over, tracing the large vein in the shaft, removing a tiny fragment of material from a fold of skin. He looked at its darker color against the rest of him and then let go of it, feeling the heaviness of it against a leg. From somewhere far off in the house he heard his name being called and turned from the mirror before he remembered that no one but himself was here.

In the morning he ate breakfast quickly, drove to a small hardware store, and loaded up his truck with several piles of tall wooden shutters for the outside windows. He got them back to the house and slid them out from the cab and leaned them against the side of the house. The sun was very warm and as he lifted each panel his arms contracted his biceps and it felt reassuring that he could do this, that as he lifted and held them in place, as he hammered the thick nails, as the wood gave way to his blows, that he was a man doing this and doing this well, that the shutters would hold, that they were lined up correctly, that the house would be better protected, that it would work, somehow all work. And when he finished and it was all done and he had showered and was sitting inside the now-darkened house holding a bottle of water, wearing a bathrobe still damp from his body, he began to cry.

He was back in his apartment and there was a man he had picked up earlier in the evening lying on his bed wearing nothing. The nude man was on his stomach and he walked over to him and placed a hand on his buttocks and the man lying there smiled warmly and groaned softly. It was a very innocent-sounding groan as if it were a young child making it and not this full-grown man. He kept his hand there and the nude man contracted a muscle and the skin suddenly went very taut and became hard and more rounded. The skin there was very warm and the man's hand seemed to take some of that heat as well. Then he took his hand and removed it and gently rolled the nude man over onto his back and stood over him. The nude man smiled once and then closed his eyes briefly and then opened them again. He rose from the bed and soundlessly left the room. The man could hear him moving about the apartment slowly. He lay down on the sheets and felt the fast-disappearing heat and smelt the pleasant odor that the nude man had left. Soon the nude man was back, wearing his clothes now, changed somehow by them, no longer that person but this new one. The man looked up at him from the bed and closed his eyes. When he opened them the newly clothed man was gone.

He was in his mother's apartment now, sitting in her kitchen and watching her cook. There was an empty plate in front of him and a napkin made of thin paper and a knife and a fork and an empty glass. He watched her poke his food with a long thin fork and turn the meat over in the pan and press down on it. She was small with a round body beneath a cotton dress. Her hair was pulled back and as she cooked she looked over at him every few moments and smiled. Then she came over to him with the pan and placed the meat on his plate and came back again with rice and beans and a Seven-Up for his glass. He sat and ate, the meat sounding very loud in his mouth and tasting of garlic and onion and salt. The almost painful fizz of the soda in his mouth with its bubbles and sweetness was very pleasant and he smiled at her and she patted his hand as if in his eating and enjoying of this food prepared by her he had made her very happy. The kitchen was small and white and old with cabinets on the walls that couldn't be closed fully because of the layers upon layers of paint applied over the years. There was linoleum on the floor that was worn away at the edges so that you could see parts of the wooden floor beneath.

He sat slightly hunched over his plate and she spoke to him in Spanish. It was about nothing and for a long while he didn't even answer her back and when he did it was just to say "yes" or "no." She kept rising and filling his glass or getting him more rice and soon he told her not to anymore because he was very full and very happy. When he said this she made a sound of disappointment as if in times past he had always been able to eat much more. He rose then and moved into the living room and it was then that the doorbell rang and her two sisters came in. They were small and round like his mother and he kissed them both and sat in an armchair and watched the three women across from him on his mother's sofa. The room was very warm and the food made him lazy and drowsy and the voices of the women, soft and almost conspiratorial, were very pleasant to him.

He thought of the train ride up here and the man he had spotted across from him. He was a boy really, with a beautiful head of black hair and a sharp, almost Roman nose. The boy's lips were slightly reddened and full and he had stared at them until the boy had noticed and smiled. The boy's body was well muscled and he stood in the rocking, swaying subway car with his arms up, resting on a bar, and his legs slightly angled so that his hips seemed turned and his torso stretched, the thin cotton material of his shirt pressed tightly against the strong-looking abdomen. The man had stared at the boy and had wanted to lift up the thin shirt and press himself against the warm, soft, brown skin and feel the young man close to him. He imagined them together, the young man coming toward him dressed in white shorts, the muscles moving beautifully beneath the skin, the boy's head tilted back and the lips parted and the teeth slightly exposed, bursts of hot air rushing over them filled with the low sounds of pleasure.

They were asking him questions now and he was answering them. His mother was serving coffee and the smell seemed everywhere in the apartment. He was sitting on the sofa and both aunts were fussing over him. They were all speaking Spanish to him and sometimes he struggled with words and he could feel his mother and aunts making eye contact with each other whenever he did so, as if this was confirming something. At the end of the questioning he got up to leave because it was getting late now and he always left after the coffee. He kissed his aunts and then his mother and walked into the kitchen and unloaded her can of garbage so that he could take it down to the basement for her and get rid of it.

She walked him to the door and he kissed her again and could see his two aunts sitting back there in the apartment waiting for her. A lamp was on now and it changed the way the room back there looked. He turned then and his mother shut the door on him and he could hear her feet moving toward the living room and then stopping. He took the stairs down into the basement and got rid of his mother's garbage and then stood there a moment. The room was long and narrow and dark and it smelled damply of aged rot. The battered metal cans stood in a row and it was very quiet and still. His heart suddenly began to beat very quickly and he turned and left the room and mounted the stairs and left the building. He walked quickly to the subway and did not stop being scared until he was home and his phone rang and someone he knew was on the other end.

That night he dreamt of his mother and his two aunts and they were trying to say something but he could not make out what it was. Then he dreamt of the boy from the train and they were on a beach together and the boy's body was very beautiful. They made love to each other and the boy held him close and kissed him deeply and when the man awoke he discovered himself with an erection that soon withered as he lay in the darkness. He knew that he was dreaming of Luquillo Beach and he forced his mind to think of other things. He lay like that for a long time but finally it worked.

Every day for a week he went back up on the train after work and walked the streets of his mother's neighborhood looking for the boy. He found him on the seventh day and the boy led him back to a small, back apartment and they made love on a thin unmade daybed that the boy slept on. He could speak only Spanish and there were papers all over the room and books and one wall was partly covered with small articles from a section out of a local Spanish newspaper called *Noticias De Tu País.* The man stared at them a moment and then looked at the boy, now naked and wrapped in loose sheets on the bed. The apartment smelled of steam heat and cooking and he could hear the muffled sounds of a television. It was far off and sounded almost underwater. The boy rose from the bed and placed the sheets down on the floor and made a pile of the other bedding. His body was not muscular as the man had thought and in bed he had been shy and unimaginative and slightly unclean.

The man watched the boy push the small pile of bedding into a corner and then began to dress. The television seemed louder now and closer and he noticed that the boy's room had the same worn linoleum as in his mother's kitchen three blocks away.

There had been a storm out at sea and it had moved quickly on shore and that was why he was back at his house on the beach. The shutters had saved the windows and there was nothing wrong with the roof or anything else that he could see. He walked around the house and then went inside, looking into each room, and decided to stay the night. He went back outside and looked up at the sky and the very dark, still clouds that seemed nailed in place there. The sea was calm but oddly colored and the man walked toward it across the great shifting piles of sand that seemed gray and forlorn now, like lumpish children told to sit still. There were bits of things in the water as if something very large and foolish had come apart, and the man pushed them about with one foot and then walked on. There seemed to be no birds anywhere and the only sound was the slow, lethargic splash of the ocean. The water seemed tentative, as if a good scolding had taken place, and the man let his feet get wet slightly. He walked on for a while, his shoulders hunched and his head down. He looked like an older man this way, someone who had fought in a war, and when he saw the body, garlanded with choking, invasive undersea vines, the only sound that came out of him wouldn't have been heard three feet away.

It was a fish, something large and powerful and now dead at his feet. Its head was swollen, the skin ripped in small uneven rows. Its eyes, round and light colored, sat in a gelatinous matter in the sockets. The fish seemed very calm lying there and the weeds made it look blanketed and elderly. It had a narrow, clever-looking mouth and the man could see small tablet-shaped teeth. Its body was very long and pale and he could imagine it under the water, rising perhaps to leap into the air and startle people in boats trying to kill it. But it was dead now.

That night he dreamt of his mother and of the boy and of the fish and then finally of Luquillo Beach. In the dream he floated high up into the air and saw the beach from there, empty and crescent shaped and very beautiful. He remained in the air, limbs outstretched as if they were wings.

He could see all of Puerto Rico as if it were a map below him with all the towns and all the regions named in English. It seemed toy-sized to him and breakable and he felt very powerful. He decided to pick the island up then and it lifted pie-like toward his now-enlarged self. He held it up to his face then and watched the minute movements of the cars and felt the vibrations from the cities and towns and, almost invisible in their tininess, the villages in the mountains. He wanted to shake the island and crush it in his hands and feel it all pulverize and he saw his new body, biceps engorged with blood and bulging cartoonishly, chest, shoulders, back, massive now, rippling with hard muscle, thighs, calves, buttocks, straining, his own phallus, erect and throbbing and cabled with veins, sticking straight out, waiting for that one moment of release. And when he did finally crush it all, his muscles flexed and working, he screamed so loudly that it woke him, pale and shivering in his empty bed.

That night he cooked for himself and the sound of his plate full of food being placed on the table seemed impossibly loud. Every bite or movement of silverware from plate to mouth seemed enlarged and mocking and he was afraid the ice cubes in his glass would slam against each other like taxis. The food was tasteless and he became angry at it, as if something in the pot had happened to it without his permission. After it was all eaten and the table cleared he lay down on his bed and opened his shirt and placed his hands on his now full, now warmed belly. He shifted his body and felt and heard liquids moving and running throughout himself. He undid his trousers and pushed them away from him and down on the floor as if they were some not-too-bright dog being punished. He then grabbed himself between the legs and felt the almost rubbery skin of his penis cradled in his fingers. He pulled on it teasingly, stretching it, and then left it alone. He rolled over then and cast off his shirt and underwear and finally the thick socks from his small feet. The sheets became rumpled and they rose up and around his body, the pillows seeming to come loose as he moved slowly about the mattress, his skin feeling very warm to him now, and there were smells from beneath his arms and his hair and from the very clean cotton of the pillowcases. He wanted to dive through it all, find some spot that would open up and let him come out onto another place. He hugged the sheets now, almost grinding himself into them, they were twisted, serpentine, thickly corded in places, he grabbed bunches of them in his fists as if they were folds of skin and pulled them down, around and toward him till the entire bed was undone and the sheets were up and covering him in their almost blinding painful whiteness.

He felt himself harden several times, his breath coming in short, tight bursts, and then, brocaded and hidden from view, kneeling there beneath the sheets, the tangle of them making his body seem something misshapen and horrible, he fell down, down, down onto the shores of Luquillo Beach in the Commonwealth of Puerto Rico.

It was nighttime and he was fourteen and slightly drunk for the first time and he was on a road with his older cousin and they were walking, barefooted, toward the beach. It was very late and the houses on either side were behind high white walls that rose up anciently, it seemed to him, and the trees hung low above the darkened road and seemed to tickle him as they walked quickly along the twisting, silkily sanded path. He could hear the dull powerful thud of waves and he followed this cousin, dark haired and taller, till they were in a grove and the wave sounds were much nearer and he could see the beach now and they were both undressing, his cousin quickly, he much slower and then they were both in the water now and the waves were lifting them dangerously higher until they were pushed up against each other or thrown deep into the warm night ocean and he was afraid sometimes and his cousin, brown and new muscled, called to him and he went over and his cousin held him close as the waves, tremendous and white foamed, pushed them up or across or under the water. And then they left the water and stood near the palm trees and he watched his cousin's body, relaxed now, still wet, insects flying near and on it, the two of them drinking some more, laughing, trying to dry off, the sand cool, some of it sticking to their skin and him watching the body across from him in the night, drunker now, his cousin moving closer, his cousin pulling him by the arm, pulling him toward a dark tangle of the twisted, coiling tree trunks, the cousin holding him like a girl, kissing him on the mouth, the cousin's hand on his shoulder, the swell of muscle and bone there, him kissing back, neck held back, the cousin seeming to want to eat him, the feel of the cousin's muscled stomach and legs and his hardened, warm dark sex and the sound of water and insects still flying and their feet scraping along the sand as the tight, close dance moved them back and around and across the dry scaled bark of the palm trees and looking up to see the sky through the thin, stalked, rattling leaves, and the ocean and the sand and the sound of his cousin's breath and his own breath as he seemed to open up like some box, just open up and speak lowly in Spanish as sound seemed to go, suspended because it was not needed at the moment and they were both arched now and taut and holding on to each other very deeply and angrily almost and then it happened and slowly the sound came back and the arching stopped and they were apart and back near their clothes and dressed and walking past the fortress-like houses and helping each other back over their own wall and through a door and up stairs and apart in small, thin cots at opposite ends of a house.

And he was gone the next day on a plane back home, in school, riding the subway, leaning against a door as a man beside him opened a newspaper and he saw in the section called *Noticias De Tu Pais* that a body had been found at Luquillo Beach. And he got off the subway and was home and his mother and two aunts were there and they were questioning him in Spanish and he sat before them, the smell of the women wrapping around him like heavy, wet arms; sweat, perfume, hairspray rising upward, incense-like, as they cried and clutched and went mad, the box closed now, lifted up and placed somewhere, and he could hear the ocean as they spoke to him, and he could see the sand and then he rose and went to his room and he could smell the ocean now and he could feel the insects and he could keep it all, all of it, here, in this room, in this building, in this city, far, far away from that beach and that island and that body.

SEXMONEYLOVE

Erasmo Guerra

As Marco walked into the bar, John came up to him, took his hand, and led him to a dark corner. A cranberry soda already waited for him. Fine, he thought; he'd drink the soda and then wander to the back to see if Jaime had come. That was why he was here, to see Jaime, not to turn a trick, and especially not to meet up with John. But here John stood, nearly pressed up against him, blocking him from the rest of the bar. Marco couldn't see past John's thinning gray hair, his bright red sweater, and the bleached bone he claimed to have found in the Chihuahua Desert. It hung from his neck like an identification tag. Marco was supposed to be impressed or flattered because his parents came from Mexico and John had guessed it immediately. None of the other johns ever had.

"I was hoping you'd come," John said, sipping a glass of wine.

"You've got plans for me?" Marco asked.

"You want me to be brutal?"

"*You* want me to be brutal," Marco said, trying to make a joke.

"No," John gushed, a simpering heat flickering across his face. "Do you want me to be brutal? You know, honest, about what I want."

Marco shrugged and took a swallow of his drink.

"Well." John hushed a bit and became serious. "I want you to come home with me tonight. To Brooklyn."

Marco nodded.

"And I want you to stay a bit longer."

"I stayed the full hour last time."

"Yes, I know," John countered, his voice fading to a nervous apology. "But you see, it's just that, well, there we were, and then zippo. You left."

"But it was an hour," Marco protested. "Maybe even an hour and a half."

"No, I know." John laughed softly. "I just need more time. I need to stretch out and relax."

"How much time do you need?"

"Well, I'd love for you to stay forever." John paused, taking a sip of his wine. "But at least, you know, overnight."

Marco shifted his weight, hoping to slip out from the corner he felt backed into, wanting to search the rest of the dim bar for Jaime. A couple of guys in jeans and leather jackets sat in the back watching the television that hung from the rafters. Jaime wasn't among them.

Marco hadn't seen Jaime in two weeks, but he would have recognized him immediately. The eyes. They crimped like fortune cookies when he smiled. He was either Chinese or Vietnamese, maybe Korean. Marco didn't know, though he was sure Jaime had a trace of Asian blood. Then again, the johns had thought the same about him. They thought he was Filipino or from another archipelago in the Asian-Pacific Ocean. They never believed he was Mexican. And nothing else. They tried to impress on him that he should at least be able to follow a tenuous and faint blood line to the ancient migrants who crossed into the Americas through the Bering Strait. He let them believe what they wanted, and said, yes, his mother was Korean, or whatever they had made up in their minds. It seemed easier. He lost himself to the peck and pull of their circling desire because it was good for money.

Marco checked his watch. It was after nine. In an hour or two, the place would fill. He hated the bar then, waiting around for a pick-up, refusing to work the johns like the other guys who made the rounds, clutching their bottled beers like their cocks, babbling to anyone who listened about how much they had made last week or last month. Three, five, seven hundred dollars a night, they'd say. Tax free. When Marco told Jaime about the scene, Jaime said he hated the sound of it too. Marco liked that. It made him think they both still had some self-respect.

"I know we had a previous arrangement," John cracked, pulling Marco out of his thoughts. "But I think it's just too high."

"What? The price?"

"Well, yes."

Marco looked around, ready to walk off and join the other guys in the back. They might be loud-mouthed hustlers, but he preferred their company over having to bargain. He didn't need to. If John didn't have the money, another john did, just as there might be another guy willing to go with John to his apartment in Brooklyn. Maybe even spend the night. Marco knew he wasn't going to do that. He felt he went for too little already.

"I think one hundred flat should do it," John said.

"One hundred and overnight?"

John nodded.

Marco had told Jaime this bar in the East Fifties was good for quick money. He forgot to warn him that the johns here liked to haggle like bargain shoppers. If he could wade through the insult of having to haggle in the first place, he could usually get a hundred fifty, which was the standard. Still, some johns balked and said they never paid more than a hundred, others not more than fifty.

Marco took a last swallow of his drink and wiped his mouth. "Sorry," he said flatly. "No sale."

John let his face hang down toward his glass. It wasn't empty, but he seemed to look at it as if he had drunk too much already. Marco took a step toward the back, but John grabbed his arm and pulled him roughly to his side.

"Oh, c'mon," he sighed. "I just got paid."

When the cab pulled up to the apartment building, Marco nearly reconsidered spending the night. The huge stone steps and the polished wood and cut-glass door at the entrance were miles from the dreariness of his own life. The building he lived in had none of the dark wood panels or rich red carpet winding around the staircase. It was quiet here, no tinny radios playing merengue or quarrels spilling out from behind rotting doors. Following John into the apartment, though, Marco saw a cockroach scrambling to one of the unlit rooms, and he remembered the place wasn't much of an improvement over his own. The paint peeled in the corners and the ceiling had a water stain. The dusty shelves were crammed with cloth-covered books. The scuffed floorboards creaked.

John sat on a piano bench he pulled into the middle of the cluttered living room. He placed Marco in front of him, between his legs, and undressed him. Marco kept looking up at the stain, trying to figure out what it looked like, but it didn't look like anything. The effort helped him get out of himself, though, and his body fell away from him like the clothes now heaped on the floor.

"Look at you," John groaned. "You're beautiful."

His breathing thickened into a series of troubled heaves. He kept grunting the word *beautiful* as if cast into the predictable drama of a telenovela. Marco kept silent and looked up at the stain.

John led Marco into the bedroom and laid him down. He felt John's hands, rough and callused, scraping against his body, tearing across his face, along his back, down to the soles of his feet. Marco did everything he had done the last time—mostly lay still.

For the first time, he thought perhaps he was paid more than what it was worth. A hundred fifty was a lot for the little he allowed, but then he knew he was more generous than most. Some guys, he heard, only got naked for a hundred fifty. Everything else was extra. For a hundred fifty, he gave his johns a round of cheap sex, even kissed those he liked, and those who whined insistently. He never loved the johns, but he let himself be loved, which was about the same to most of them in those desperate hours. Still, in this room now, looking at the spotty mirror across the dimness, Marco watched himself guiltily, his torso rising up from the tiny bed, legs open wide, John's head bobbing between his thighs.

When the hour sputtered out, Marco got up and dressed himself to leave. He wanted to head back to the bar. He knew it would be packed, a doorman probably stationed at the front, charging a cover, but he wanted to go anyway, see if Jaime had shown. John lay in his bed, burrowing under the cover of his sheets. He refused to get up. He told Marco to show himself out and shut the door behind him.

The subway train pulled into the Lexington stop, and as Marco waited for the doors to open, he spotted Jaime across the platform. At first, he thought it a trick, his body drunk with desire. This wasn't Jaime, just someone who looked like him. Marco nearly dismissed the guy until he got a better look at the face, the flash of those eyes before they turned to the track for the next downtown train. Marco crept up behind Jaime with the thought of pushing aside the dark wave of hair and kissing the smooth nape of his neck, a compromise for wanting to kiss him on the mouth. The fluorescent lights discouraged everything, though, and he reminded himself that nothing was real yet. He was still walking around with Jaime's name in his shoe—a *brujería* he believed got Jaime to call him in the first place.

"So," Marco whispered into Jaime's ear. "You found the bar?"

Jaime spun around, a smirk flashing across his face. "I found it. You going over there?"

"Nothing else to do," Marco offered.

"I'm hanging it up for tonight."

"Going home?"

Jaime nodded, distracted by an approaching train.

Marco tried to choke down his silent disappointment, but it lodged itself in the back of his throat. He needed a glass of water, a sloppy kiss, anything to unravel the chalky lump.

When the train came to a stop, Jaime got in. Marco remained on the platform. He wanted to go in after Jaime, but his legs felt weak, as if the slightest movement would send him stumbling flat onto the concrete. He shoved his hands into his pockets to keep them still. The wad of money John had given him was there. He traced the edges of a few bills with his fingers. He would have used it all to have Jaime. Of course, he hoped that even if he made the offer, Jaime would decline the money. This was what all the johns hoped.

The conductor called for the closing doors, and Marco, without saying another word, afraid the proposition might fall from his mouth and earn him nothing but rejection, put a loose fist to his ear in the shape of a phone. Call, he wanted to say. Jaime understood and nodded as the doors shut between them and the train rumbled down the dark shaft of the tunnel. Marco turned and headed toward the bar, his loneliness like that of the night clerk of the subway token booth, to whom no one paid much attention, or bothered with, who was probably locked in from the outside and had no choice but to sit under the harsh light and wait out the night.

The Europe of Their Scars

RANE ARROYO

Two tourists fish in Portugal, their secret wounds healing. Their love of one woman hurries them home (a hotel), but the river in which they whispered all day long follows them. Their woman is at church, mermaid among saints. Vicente and Carlos whisper in a bar without a jukebox. They look like lovers to their lover when she arrives, breathless with her love of God. She is each man's true love, but that matters little to her, as it shouldn't. Carlos and Vicente accept her ghost and the three of them sit in alcohol's silences. As they stagger to their room, the river replaces the fish that the men imagine catching in their minds. They don't love her. Europe is full of women and the two friends have each other. They drink all night in their room and watch the sun rise over the Europe that must accommodate their desires, whatever they are. They make love to each other and it is a surprise, that despite the years of knowing each other, they are each still mysterious. In the morning, they shave at the same sink, but say nothing. Nuns and priests would understand such private vows.

Ten years later, Vicente writes a letter to the dozing moon. He sends it by smoke, and returns to the wreckage of his weekend. He spills cigarettes on the stairs. Sits on the floor in his briefs. And waits. Is he in Paris again, if only by spirit? Doesn't it matter at all to his dazed soul? He lets the phone ring because his messiah will not have a voice. Wants for a friend, anyone, to read Shelley aloud to him. His beard draws him to morning. That trip to Europe changed his life, or consumed it. And now? He signs the letter by spilling wine over his chest.

In Italy, the one fed by the silk route, Vicente and Carlos see a slow life that's not theirs. From the gondola, the world seems church-dark. Arm in arm, they become tourists once again. The prosaic, under moonlight, proves malleable to the youth of the men's Venice. The coherent tides take them to a dawn without souvenirs. Exteriors of bedrooms shine with spilled wine. Masqueraded mysteries go home. Then noon, time for tuxedos, formal ape hour for yet another occasion. They stop to look at the sea, but Vicente and Carlos know it's too cold to swim in it or to belong to it. It's time to go back to colder climates, back to unstoppable weddings. Carlos wants to kiss in a doorway but Vicente isn't sure that God created lust to tempt mankind. Love, insists Carlos, sends the blood from the head to the cock. He holds Vicente's compass but the two men remain lost. They enter the currents of other humans and arrive at a party wearing identical frowns.

Carlos is exhausted by Barcelona's well-dressed dead at the discos. They beg him for breath, any slow kiss he can offer them. Men and women circle him, each one with valid reasons for a season in Carlos's mouth. The church bells swing from left ear to right ear. The drunk matador lifts his shirt to prove he has no scars. Then it's Carlos's turn: the crowd hushes. What do they see? Like any other gentleman, he borrows a cigarette from the suicide next to him. Carlos blows rings that turn Earth into Saturn. He bows to the applause. The bar mirror is used to miracles. The party returns to its pose as a mock constellation. Spanish women offer comforts that are beyond Carlos's particular pain, but how beautiful they are in their casualness, cruelty. He loves them today; what day is it? Friends are off getting high, but Carlos is an audience member of the try-outs for the newest Eve. Where is Vicente?

In London, a naked painter gives Vicente a tour of his "mistakes." And they are many: a pile of canvases, a landslide of colors. Then the men sit under an olive tree to talk about destiny as a shrug. The naked painter. Vicente in his expensive pants. Later in the week, the novelist is a tourist, if only to develop calluses on his camera eye. In the church, a dragon blows fire from the other side of stained-glass veils. A young existentialist eyes Vicente, and they go off into the ruins of a good wine. Vicente feel the wings of the dragon rush him down an ashy path. This is a moment of an important decision. He did not come to Europe to become a bitter man. He makes love like a matador, a terrifying night of power.

Carlos drinks wine in Dante Plaza in Copenhagen, not named for a poet but a knuckle fighter with unusually big hands. The pigeons try to peck out the sun's eyes in a foolish attempt to make blindness normal. Vicente's papers scatter, find exile in a cloud; he is left wordless. Time to rent an airplane and a handsome pilot to get a bird's-eye view of the city; but first more wine, blood of an unlived day. Vicente's novel has to be *novel,* or he has wasted these drunk nights with the moon. A violinist collapses in a chair at the two men's table and they nod at each other, strangers linked by the geography of individual pain. The violinist thinks they are lovers but Vicente and Carlos have been arguing. Each of them go home with someone else, and in the morning they laugh at their foolishness. They shave together after their guests leave. Then they become lovers, body and soul.

In a French cafe, an American bluesman wails for the heartsick in this sea-blue night. The saxophone speaks all the languages of the light in the slow sky over the living. Vicente gets homesick for an America that doesn't exist. His cigarettes send smoke signals to God, from whose corpse has sprung this Parisian primitivism. Carlos makes a mental note to stop thinking so much and to just enjoy the ruins of his present reality. The bluesman is sad about a lover who may or may not be real. An unshaved, unwashed, and unhurried Vicente stares at this performing, unbared soul in all of its true ugliness, or at least as much as he can without going blind. Carlos wonders what it would be like to be happy with a woman, but the moment passes, and soon he's gossiping with the drunk moon.

French museums crowd the mind with the stolen relics of Homo Sapiens across time and space. The headless statues of young Greeks reject evolution, for they are timeless, never changing, stuck in poses. It is difficult to imagine anyone's destiny being different than one's own. Carlos stays there long enough to be able to have a story or two for friends at home. He is asked to buy hashish, but Vicente isn't interested in blurring the world he is now responsible for because of his claim of words. Soon he is late for an appointment, skips it. Watches men watch him. They think Vicente is a spy, sexy but carnivorous. He wears the morning beard of the unpublished. The novelist looks around him and Europe is invisible; he could be anywhere. Where was his best friend, Carlos? Why did the world exist only when they were together? But the two friends had agreed to meet at Campagna beach in three weeks, and each went alone to the Europe offered in their personalized condom ads. Vicente had his first wet dreams and they were odd, the way the ocean is when it tugs at your ankles. It is both an invitation and a trap.

Three weeks later, they met once again, only on the beach, swimming until it got too cold to be naked and waited for something, someone, anything to return them to life before passports. Being displaced is also about having too many new places from which to choose. Being in love is worse than not being in love. The friends stayed on that beach as long as they could and then flew home with the extra weight of tears in their suitcases. As the two men lost contact with each other in an America of shouting pitchmen, they grew feverish in their quietness. Vicente never finished his novel. Carlos grew to be nervous about being naked before anyone but God. Were they as handsome as they seem in surviving photographs taken in the Europe of their scars?

Dialéctica del Amor / Dialectics of Love

Francisco X. Alarcón

Words of Warning

For me poetry is a necessity, a mystery, an enigma like life, and like love. For me poetry has no rules. Like love, poetry comes to me unexpectedly, without much warning. Experience has taught me to respect and cherish these rare and mysterious poetic moments in which words somehow regain their ancient power and make us wonder and ponder once again.

In poetry, words shed their disguises, run naked, can kiss you in the mouth, bite you in the ear, become tender flowers but also piercing arrows. The best poems are almost always a paradox open to interpretation. Unassuming poetic lines sometimes contain explosive bombs. Poetry makes you vulnerable; most lovers know this. Maybe this is why poetry has been the preferred tongue of lovers since the beginning of time. In Latino culture the true narrative *del amor,* of love, is found not in printed texts but in heart-felt popular songs, *las baladas y las canciones populares*—the wise *poesía del pueblo,* the poetry of our people.

It's about time to acknowledge that there is a rich gay Latino and Hispanic sensibility at the core of this poetic and musical tradition. Who can now contest that contemporary Mexican popular musical expression really revolves around the sun-like genius of Juan Gabriel, who is widely thought to be gay? Or that the greatest poet in the Spanish language in the twentieth century, Federico García Lorca, was gay?

But since poetry is the language of prophets and visionaries, who are mostly dissenters and troublemakers, writing poetry in critical times becomes a dangerous undertaking that could lead its practitioners to persecution, imprisonment, exile, disappearance, or death, like in the case of García Lorca and many poets in Latin America.

The feminist movement has taught me that the personal is political, that even the most intimate experience—as that epiphany commonly dismissed as an orgasm—has social and political implications. This seems an easy proposition to accept and follow, but it takes more than courage to speak the unspeakable, to say what has remained unsaid for so long. This lesson in courage and guts, in defiance and spirit, I learned from a group of very strong women, most of them Chicana lesbians, like Gloria Anzaldúa, Cherrie Moraga, Carla Trujillo, and Esther Hernández, among others.

I see my poetry both as a celebration of life and as a challenge to silence and death. The poems included here come from a section I have titled *"Dialectica del amor/Dialectics of Love"* and are part of an unpublished book of poems. Since the end of the Cold War, and with the disappearance of the Communist threat, we Chicanos, undocumented workers, and Latino immigrants seem to increasingly be given the role of society's scapegoats, the easy targets, the unwelcome outsiders, the internal enemies.

Of course, homophobia and AIDS have only made this process of singling out even more distressing to Chicano/Latino gay males. This is the life-and-death context of this collection of poems. I confess—as an unrepentant and repeat linguistic offender and outlaw breaker of the English-only rule imposed by the vanishing majority and enforced by most editors in our Spanish-sounding state of California—that I wrote these poems in Spanish and English with the criminal intent of publishing them in *both* languages. You are my judges.

Dialéctica del amor

para el mundo
no somos nada
pero aquí juntos
  tú y yo
somos el mundo

Dialectics of Love

to the world
we are nothing
but here together
  you and I
are the world

Para nosotros

no hay
palabras

por eso
al encontrarnos

a veces
se nos hace

nudo
la garganta

For Us

there are
no words

that's why
sometimes

when we meet
a knot

ties up
our throat

Noches frías

sonríes
sonrío:
innecesaria
la calefacción

Cold Nights

you smile
I smile—
no need
for a heater

Elocuentes

en silencio
nuestras manos
se ponen a platicar

Eloquent

all quiet
our hands do
`all the talking

Caliente

comienzas
a apuntar
al cielo

Horny

you start
pointing
to the sky

Eros

no hay
llave
para tu
puerta

sólo
lengua
para tu
cerradura

Eros

there is
no key
for your
door

only
a tongue
for your
keyhole

Mordiéndome

las orejas
me susurras:
"cálmala
tonto"

Biting

my ears
you whisper:
"take it easy
you fool"

Cigarros

ardemos
cada uno
en la boca
del otro

Cigarettes

we burn
in each
other's
mouth

Clímax

de pronto
en la punta
de la lengua
¡una galaxia!

Climax

suddenly
on the tip
of our tongue
a galaxy!

Talento natural

"no soy
poeta"
me cuentas

después
de un gran
poema vergón

Natural Talent

"I'm not
a poet"
you tell me

after
a great
fucking poem

Continente	**Continent**
ahora resultas ser continente	now you turn out to be a continent
me puedo pasar la vida	I can spend my whole life
y nunca acabar de explorarte	and never will I finish exploring you

Conocimiento común	**Common Knowledge**
yo sé tú sabes todos saben	I know you know everybody knows
y aún así nadie parece saber	and yet nobody seems to know

Bendiciones

tus ojos
me han hecho
ver otra vez

tus manos
me han enseñado
a acariciar

tus brazos
me han mostrado
cómo abrazar

todas
las maravillas
de tu cuerpo

me han devuelto
la esperanza
y la alegría

las bendiciones
de los sentidos
y del alma

Blessings

your eyes
have made me
see again

your hands
have taught me
how to caress

your arms
have shown me
how to embrace

all
the wonders
of your body

have given me
back hope
and joy

the blessings
of the senses
and the spirit

Callejeros

sólo
estos perros
saben

del dolor
de las calles
a oscuras

mientras
en las casas
crujen camas

ellos afuera
rastrean
el olvido

los rebeldes
de siempre
los desolados

no ladran
ni gruñen
a los ladrones

lo contrario:
chisguetean
los muros

de los bancos
las iglesias
los hoteles

Street Dogs

only
these dogs
know about

the grief
of streets
after dark

while
beds squeak
inside homes

they trace
oblivion
outside

forever
rebellious
desperadoes

they don't bark
nor growl
at thieves

au contraire—
they spray
the walls

of banks
churches
hotels

Proscriptos

qué decir
ante
el silencio

las páginas
que se quedan
sin escribir

los libros
en donde
todavía

ni somos
ni estamos
ni existimos

esta vida
condenada
a la nada

aquí
nadie sabe
ni sabrá

del mar
que llevamos
adentro

Outcasts

what to say
about
silence

the pages
left
unwritten

the books
in which
we are yet

to be
to appear
to exist

this life
condemned
to nothingness

here
nobody knows
nor will know

of the sea
we carry
within us

del fuego	of the fire
que encendemos	we ignite
con el cuerpo	with our bodies
del	from
otro lado	the other side
de la noche	of night
aquí seguimos:	here we remain
proscriptos	—outcasts
por vida	for life

Ritual de desamor

el hombre
arrojó
una piedra
al río

la piedra
se hundió
al fondo
como su amor

el hombre
se retiró
y se fue
por el camino

más tarde
en el bolsillo
la misma piedra
se encontró

Ritual for Unloving

the man
threw
a stone
to the river

the stone
sank to
the bottom
as his love

the man
then left
and took
the road

later
in his pocket
he found
the same stone

En la boca

me queda
ay todavía
ese amargo
sabor tuyo

In My Mouth

I still have
oh that lingering
bitter taste
of you

Blues del SIDA

casi todos
nuestros amigos
de San Francisco
ya se han ido

no más postales
no más llamadas
no más lágrimas
no más risas

silencio y nieblina
ahora oscurecen
nuestro antes asoleado
Distrito de la Misión

dondequiera
que ahora vamos
sólo somos un par
de extraños

AIDS Blues

almost all
our friends
in San Francisco
nowadays are gone

no more cards
no more calls
no more tears
no more laughs

silence and fog
now darken
our once sunny
Mission District

everywhere
we now go
we're just a pair
of strangers

Plegaria del desierto

montañas:
abuelas
olvidadas
y recordadas

concédannos
su aliento
su fuerza
su salud

para aliviarnos
uno a otro
como la noche
las heridas

Desert Prayer

mountains—
grandmothers
forgotten
and recalled

grant us
your breath
your strength
your health

to soothe
like the night
each other's
wounds

Frontera

ninguna
frontera
podrá
separarnos

Border

no
border
can ever
separate us

Locas

Secret Dirty Self

D. L. Alvarez

Susan's date folded himself over. *Look what I can do.* He pulled his thighs down toward his face, his chin scrunched into the top of his chest, his stomach accordioned along the creases of his abdomen, and his asshole stared straight up at the ceiling. "That's so cute," said Susan. *Cute.* A word so overused it had lost its meaning, like *love.* Except cute was a word that, due to its meaninglessness, could be used on any occasion when the more appropriate word wasn't appropriate. Love, because its meaning was lost, was a word never used unless coated thickly with irony. *That's so, er,* cute, *I* love *it.*

Pink knees boxed his ears and his large feet smushed a pillow way up at the head of the bed. On the night stand a digital clock blinked red: 9:59, 10:00. It was Monday, and much of San Francisco was already asleep.

The night they met she wore the white dress I made for her, which fits snugly, showing off her thin waist and fleshy behind. They were in a bar crowded with people who just gotten out of the studio theater across the street, most of them regretting or justifying the fifteen dollars spent on tickets. I'd seen the show in previews and had warned Susan, but we were obligated because this girl we work with was A.D.

"Thank God I got a comp," said Susan to the man who bought her a gin and tonic. "My friend, Nadine, is assistant director—*What was that, Nadine?*" After the performance Nadine was running around backstage. Susan gave her the thumbs-up, then pointed to her watch like, *Great job, but gotta go....* Fifteen minutes later she had trashed everything from the premise to the backdrops. *And that suit didn't fit any better than his accent.* All this with a total stranger. Except, not total. The man was a singer, famous enough that she recognized him. He complimented her on her outfit, noting how striking the smooth white fabric was against her long black hair, and because he was a celebrity Susan became more self-conscious than usual. She thought, *Is Kirk Ivy into Japanese girls? Does Kirk Ivy think I'm easy because of the way I'm dressed? When Kirk Ivy laughs is it because he finds me clever, or just silly?*

The next morning she and Kirk Ivy ate breakfast naked, standing up, him behind her. North Beach was a postcard view from his Barbie's Townhouse, the script on the back of his business card reading, *This is too easy.* When Susan spilled some milk on the hardwood floor she immediately apologized, saying, "...Your apartment is so clean. It's like you, you're so clean." He led her down the hall to the water closet, took her in, and latched the door. The room was full of religious kitsch, and sitting on the toilet placed him at the center of a busy altar.

"You're going to be the prisoner of my secret dirty self," he said, and let out a high-pitched fart. Susan squealed. She played at fumbling at the latch as if fighting to escape a toxic fume. As the latch clicked open she heard a turd drop in the bowl. They both laughed as she continued her routine, crawling down the hall with one hand at her throat, fake-coughing. "Run, run!" he cried, "Hide where you will, I'll always find you, ha-ha-ha!"

It wasn't until she related this story to me over the phone that the full irony hit her; she saw a man who had gone to lengths to echo the look and sounds of Elvis, sitting on a toilet. "In a funny way," she said, "it was kind of sexy—the Graceland thing aside."

"Are you gonna sell-out?" I asked. *Selling-out* was our code phrase for falling in love, because it meant you would enter the sanctioned world of the couple, and would stay home watching *sell-out* videos instead of sparking revolution in the streets—not that we did that either, but some of our friends did, so we took credit by association. If one of us saw a guy we liked, we'd say, "I can hardly wait to sell-out!"

A few weeks later it became clear she was falling for him when she started relating their phone chats word for word. "He called from Boston, and asked me if I had Prince Albert in a can, y'know. Well I told him, yes, he's in a fucking can. When can he come out? And he, he's in this 7-11 or Quick Stop or whatever, and the phone must be right near the register because I can hear the clerk ringing people up, and he's talking all dirty, saying things like, 'Oh, he's coming out, baby; he's pushing at the door right now; if I don't let him out he's gonna break it down,' y'know. It was so funny." But in my mind the funny thing was how she'll turn right around and try to be casual about the whole thing—like, "Isn't it a joke how simple-minded this famous guy is?"

Susan always poked fun at girls who date guys from bands, and so she volunteered explanations as to how her situation was different. "He's on tour most of the time, so it's easy, and the sex is great. Plus, I'm hardly a groupie. Did I tell you Nadine called? I wasn't home, she left a message on my machine. *Is he really as hung as they say?* Click. She's mad at me because I didn't tell her myself. But tell her what? That I'm seeing Kirk Ivy? It's not like he's my boyfriend, you know. I mean, yes, it's been four months since we met, but if you add up the actual time we've had together it's not even a week. Plus, Nadine would just give me shit about the time I teased her for buying one of his CDs."

At this, Susan's shoulders slumped and she bit her lower lip. "What am I going to do? He's fun, he really is, but his music sucks. It SUCKS!"

When he returned from tour he took her away for a few weeks. I fed her cat and read the postcards she sent from hotels and road stops, photographs of carpeted lobbies with nobody in them and one of Main Street, Stockton, California, Kirk's hometown. Sometimes two or three came in a day, with two-sentence sentiments: *We have nothing in common! It's a setup for a sell-out. / He only reads magazines... I'll let you draw in the quote marks. / His mother calls me "oriental."* This last one on the backside of a picture of Jerry Lewis wearing buck teeth, a long braid, and eyeliner accentuating his "slanted" eyes.

In one of the Stockton motels she woke him with a hand job. Afterward, she lay across him and drew curlicues in the cum on his shoulder. Some of it dotted the pillow, and one thick tear ran down his cheek. Susan loved watching his face when he came. He seemed so surprised each time, like he didn't know *that* would happen. As she doodled, the morning light picked up a glint from her fingernails, which were freshly manicured. That had been his idea. Something they did the day before while shopping in an endless mall with one of his cousins. On the wall of Lady Nails was a chart of long fake nails ranging from hot pink to a muddy red, many of them ornamented with decals of stripes, rosebuds, and unicorns. Kirk spoke with a woman who worked there as if he doubted her English, as if this environment were foreign. "*French* manicure. You know this?" "Sure, sure," she nodded, "French." He searched the small shop in vain for an example of what he was talking about. He added, "It's very subtle." "Yes, yes, very *nice*," she said, as if in opposition. The woman in the chair next to Susan was having the word *sunshine* painted on the nail of her ring finger. It was part of a haiku she had written about her boyfriend.

"Go on now," said Susan to Kirk, "ladies only." And at this he actually blushed. Once he left, the manicurist grabbed Susan's shoulder. "That's him, the singer!" "No," Susan lied, "but they are related."

Because they used a Mother of Pearl gloss instead of clear, the cum matched her nails. The greasy aroma of pancakes and bacon from the Denny's next door mixed with the odor of sex. Kirk asked what she was thinking. Susan smeared a dab of cum on the end of his nose and said, "Sunshine."

In a Mustang he had bought for his brother, the two of them drove up the coast. They meant to rediscover nature after a weekend of being among the unnatural. Everything in Stockton was a testament to things man-made: swirls of plastic gold on fake-wood paneling, girls dressed like gifts in shiny clothes with huge bows. Kirk's mother, Vera, was perturbed when Susan asked for a glass of water. "Oh," said Vera, "We have Pepsi, Sprite, orange soda..."

"Water is fine, really. I *like* water."

"Are you sure you don't want some ginger ale? We have Snapple, I bet you like that." Finally she gave in and set Susan down on a vinyl sofa, in front of a mammoth television, with a glass of ice water and a coaster. Then she and her son disappeared somewhere into the back of the house. On the screen a man with thin black hair and Bermuda shorts was complaining to a studio audience about his thoughtless roommate, who was also his ex-girlfriend. As he spoke they showed the so-called ex-girlfriend in a small box imposed at the upper-left-hand corner of the screen negating everything he said with wild shakes of her head. She appeared to be translating his testament for the conceptually impaired, melting it down into one idea: lies. Susan flicked the power button at the base of the screen, which cast the image into white snow, but somehow the ex-boyfriend's whiny voice still came through, saying, "It's like she does it just to irritate me, y'know? She never made sounds like that when we were together."

A moment later, Vera returned with a glass dove brimming with pastel mints. "Make yourself comfortable. Kirk and I are catching up." She picked up a handful of remote controls and aimed them at different spots in the room until the picture and voices were back in sync. "We have cable and HBO," she said, handing Susan the thinnest remote. "This one changes channels, but don't turn it off. It's hooked into the stereo and the cable box, and there's a certain order you have to go in, otherwise it can get really screwed up. I barely understand it myself." She forced a smile, then started to leave again.

"Vera," Susan called, "Maybe you should just turn it off, then. I have a paperback out in the car..."

"Look at the *Guide*," said Vera with some irritation. She meant *TV Guide*, the only thing on the coffee table besides the mints. Shuffling down the hall, she called over her shoulder, "I think *A League of Their Own* is on today."

"That film with Madonna and Gena Davis? Isn't that too dated for HBO?" I asked.

"Well, it could've been on anything, they get a million channels," she called back to me. "But obviously, it's some sort of crack at the modern *oriental* girl. Know what I mean?" Her whole tone was, oh here's this *women's interest* film, *you* would probably like that. I wonder if she knows her son fucked Madonna in London. Not recently; this was back before Lourdes and Evita and all that. But she just showed up at his hotel at 3 a.m. and said, "*I'm lonely.*"

"Madonna's an infamous size queen," I said. "Warren Beattie, Sean Penn, Dennis Rodman, that trainer guy, all her boyfriends have been hung."

"Right, I'm sure that was the bottom line, but according to Kirk——and this could just be his naive interpretation—she was sincerely distraught. Not that you can't be both lonely *and* a size-queen out to kill two birds with one shlong."

"We've all been there."

"He says she just walked in, this sad tiny woman—that's how he described her—and sat down on the edge of the bed, sort of pathetic. But not too pathetic to fuck. Poor little Madonna. I watched about an hour of that damn movie. Every time she came on, I just imagined this interpreter in a box in the upper-left-hand corner of the screen underscoring all her lines by shaking her head and telling us, 'What the Queen of Pop is really trying to say here is, *she's lonely.*'"

From this Susan segued directly into asking how my date went with the guy I met at Nadine's birthday party, a student of microbiology. I resented the train of thought but kept this to myself, confessing that the date had been canceled, with only the vaguest enthusiasm toward a follow-up date. "It's fine," I said. "He's kinda young and kinda prissy, and both in a boring way."

The experienced whore / leans into the car window / Her perfume / pervades the cab as a fantastic promise / Skirt lifts with habit / familiar, trustworthy, bored / South of Eureka / the aged redwood / carved out at its base / straddles a convoy of tricks.

"God help me. I've started writing poetry. At least they're not love poems, but how far away am I? The only people who write poems are hippies, lovers, and the lovelorn. I'm not a fucking hippie! And I don't want to be in or out of love—gross! I am, though. God help me, I'm falling in love with a man I don't fully respect. Have I gotten kinder with age, or more desperate?"

"You're not kinder."

"Yeah."

"But maybe those aren't the only two options."

She showed me her journal, which was indeed infested with a plague of poems. "This one is about the Drive Thru Tree. See? *The aged redwood…straddles a convoy of tricks.* Do you like that light touch? I was thinking of calling it *Drive Thru Tree.*" She told me about their trip north, snaking up the Redwood Highway, stopping at roadside shops to look at burlwood lamps, smoked fish, and dollhouse wicker furnishings. She showed some poems to Kirk, who just laughed.

"The tree is a hooker?" he had asked.

"Well, nature…nature is *an experienced whore.*"

"You've been in the city too long," he had said.

"He's right," said Susan to me. "I approach nature as if it were a constructed amusement. If we went any distance from the marked trails, bathrooms, and gift shops, I grew nervous. Why am I like that? I really wanted to be this gung-ho, feisty-camper grrrrl."

I reminded her of her last long-term relationship, "That's not the girl you are that's the girl you admire."

"Yes," she said, and then sighed. "That's the girl I fall for. So I thought, *I'll be her, and then Kirk will fall for me.*"

"But, he already has."

She nodded. I've watched Susan go through this frustration before. She has an incredible spirit and will, and doesn't understand why that doesn't make her a little butch-er in the face of adventure. She would brave the outback in a minute if it were just a matter of endurance. But she's a sissy when it comes to unknowables. You can't practice the outback.

This makes her grateful for sex. If not an adventurer, she can at least be naughty. And Kirk, more than any previous lover, appreciates that, encourages it. *Who's my little girl? What mischief is she up to?*

I loved to hear her sex stories, mainly because he's a celebrity. It's fun to see someone's picture in a magazine and know tons of intimate crap about them that the average reader doesn't have access to. They were always trying something kinky—nothing extreme, but more than you'd guess by the looks of either of them: spanking, semipublic sex, hot wax. But what made it work, Susan said, was Kirk's intensity, his awe of her body and its functions.

One day they hiked up a grassy hill in Oregon. They drank beers with their lunch, and Kirk made her laugh so hard she started to pee. She pleaded with him to stop joking, saying, "Stop, you're making me pee!." And you'd think she had just stumbled onto the precipice of a great theory. He took her in his arms and stared at her intently.

"You have to pee," he said.

"Yes, I do."

"No, you don't understand." He maneuvered his right leg between hers, lifted her skirt with one hand, and with the other on her ass pressed her against him until most of her weight rested on this leg and repeated, "You *have* to pee."

His eyes were her favorite thing about him. They were capable of demanding and pleading at once, of reaching into her and opening up for her. Whenever he asked her to do something—asked with his eyes—she felt compelled to respond. But in this case, she wasn't sure she could. The physical position he put her in was uncomfortable. He lifted her some so that she had to stand on tip-toe. If he lost his grip or his footing on the slope of this hill, she had no way to keep from falling. Also, she wondered if he really knew what he was asking for. Kirk had an almost zenlike ability to live in the now, which was Susan's polite version of describing a man incapable of seeing the consequences of his actions. So she wondered if he knew that if she peed on him, he'd wear the mark of it all the way back down the hill, past the picnickers in the valley, who could easily recognize him, and into the parking lot full of weekend travelers.

"Do it," he ordered. And her body complied with a healthy flood, soaking her panties, his pant leg, his sock and shoe while his face took on that now-familiar deer-in-headlights wonderment, as if he couldn't believe *this* was happening.

I like these stories, but at the same time I resent them. I resent how they've taken the place of the stories Susan and I used to tell each other, which weren't stories so much as just a cycle of longing and rejection and longing again. We always went for normal-looking guys who were inevitably freaked out by our "wild" lifestyles (read: junky furniture, too many books, and the inability to suppress boredom). Now she has a normal-looking guy who appreciates her, and I feel some unspoken pressure to mirror her as I did before. It's in the way she sometimes hesitates a few moments before spilling the goods. The pause is new between us, and I worry about what will grow there. I sense Susan wishes I too had a boyfriend so that we could both gush and she wouldn't have to feel like she sold out alone.

But *selling out* is beginning to loose its charm for me. I spend more time with our revolutionary friends, the activists and world-changers. They bombard me with all the crap that goes on, the injustices and power-imbalance. In the light they shed, love looks like a conspiracy—not the emotion itself, but the way it's played out. The way we focus obsessively on love, spending every ounce of time that isn't consumed by the work week in search of it; it's dirty and selfish. Of course these words, the ones in the last few sentences, aren't mine yet. I'm just trying them out. My secret is that I'm entertaining the idea of falling in love with one of the rebels. My secret dirty self would like to be the muse for a Jewish anarchist filmmaker with romantic and powerful ideas about the capacity of art to evoke social change. Or maybe I'll move to Mexico City and spin records for the revolution (certainly nothing by Susan's lover). Is blind love also deaf?

One night I ran into Susan at the bar where she met Kirk. He had just taken a car service to the airport, but before he went away she finger-fucked him to the Dropkick Murphy's CD I bought her on Valentine's Day. She had never penetrated a lover before Kirk, assuming the nervous boys she usually dated would feel too implicated in such queer pleasure. But Kirk didn't worry about his image with Susan. At times he was downright fey. She figured it was because his image is already out in the world. And it's not even *his* image, but an imitation of an icon in his youth: the early Elvis, a strong chin and soft eyes. It's an image so solid even Elvis himself couldn't bring it down, try as he did. The music was loud enough to shake them with its boisterous melody. Kirk's eyes rolled up in his head and he let out the stuttered hum of an antique vibrator, while she kept the rowdy tempo inside him.

Early on, before either of them knew much about the other, Kirk showed her a trick. He said, "Look what I can do." Then he lay down on the bed with this whopping hard-on, flipped his legs over his head, pressed his chin into the top of his chest, and lowered the erection into his own mouth. Susan might have been taken aback some, but they had just spent the last twenty-four hours together without sleep, and the sight of him collapsed into himself was more surreal than shocking.

"What did you do?" I asked my friend.

"What *could* I do? I applauded. He got more of it down than I could."

Crazy Horse Memoirs

Emanuel Xavier

We woke up naked on the floor of Paul's Manhattan College dorm after a wild night at Limelight. We'd just convinced him to drive us to the Bronx Zoo when, SLAM!—we drove right into another car that was trying to make an illegal turn. When he announced he was going back to the dorm, we got out of the car, carrying on like the queens we were, reading him to filth.

"I told him not to take that U-turn!"

"Uh-huh, girlfriend! He shoulda listened!"

"That's right! He needs to go back to Kansas!"

Stopping to buy the closest thing to liquid crack, a forty-ounce Crazy Horse beer, it was off to the Bronx Zoo—strollin'...no, not strollin'...clickin'. Yeah, that's right! Clickin'. Click-click-clickin' our imaginary high heels through the zoo, carrying on all loud and shit so that the boys would notice us and pay homage.

Our first exhibit: the men's bathroom, where I placed a quarter hit of acid with South Park's Kenny in each of our hands like it was the body of Christ, downing it with Crazy Horse. Sal, busy tagging his name and number on the bathroom door, realizing it was already there—the words "Sal is a whore" written over them. Sal adding *"and much much more"* before we split.

The drugs made us feel like we had just stepped into the wildest nightlife we'd ever seen—no glass separating us from the many bats and other strange nocturnal creatures lurking throughout the club. The wicked sounds of darkness filled the air while we reminisced about the many hours we had spent together on some New York City dance floor. Chris and I had fallen in love underneath pinlights and spotlights. Flying and crawling all over the place, this clientele, though, was too much for Sal, who began screaming from deep in his hallucination:

"*AY, DIOS MIO!* THE BATS! THEY'RE ALL OVAH DA PLACE! THEY'RE GONNA BITE ME! THEY'RE GONNA BITE ME!"

"*Loca*...pleeease! You're making a scene!" I yelled as Chris and I proceeded to haul his ass out of the exhibit, concerned that security would find out and take our best friend away.

The sudden burst of sunlight and the heightened sensitivity of our acid trip made our skin feel like it was being burnt right off. We were blinded and Sal was struck with instant paranoia. He ran away from us as fast as he could, as if running for the border.

"I CAN SEE THE LIGHT! IT'S THE END OF THE WORLD! I SEE THE LIGHT!"

Chasing after him, we dispersed into the crowd awaiting an exciting journey through the jungles of the world on the Bengali Express. Once the ride was over, we unanimously agreed that we'd all had more fun on the Long Island Expressway.

This was when the acid hit hard and we first spotted the flying monkeys stalking us from behind ominous trees swirling into human faces.

"Yo, I think we're, like, seriously baked!"

"You think?" Sal asked vacantly. Chris, freaking out, became convinced he was being punished for stealing that Spice Girls lollipop from Mr. Soto's bodega on the Concourse. Intoxicated with love, I felt his genuine fear endearing him to me.

"Don't worry, papi! I'll protect you!" I declared in my manliest tone, locking eyes with him.

"With what? Your purse?" Sal mocked, admirably maintaining his sense of humor.

Following a trail that led to a set of life-size metal rhinoceroses, we spotted Latasha LaBeija—huge-assed pre-op transsexual from the House of LaBeija, looking bigger than ever and trying to mount one of the statues for a photo op. Wouldn't you just know that Chris climbed up the other—vogueing, queening out, and battling Latasha in legendary poses like he was doing a fashion spread for Giorgio Armani? Sal and I cheered and applauded deliriously like two queens at a ball. Meanwhile, Latasha struggled to get on top while tourists stopped to take advantage of this non-designated Kodak moment.

"Next time I see you at the piers, I'ma cut you!" Latasha yelled. Jumping off, Chris joined us in drug-enhanced infectious laughter before we split, leaving Latasha behind, wounded in front of her friends.

Fucked up on acid, we walked around aimlessly for hours. By the time we realized we were exhausted, it was five-thirty, and the zoo was closing. Clickin' our heels ALL THE WAY back to the Fordham Road entrance, we watched as the animals packed their bags. Polar bears with huge paws cartoonishly waved, "Good-bye, girrrls! C-ya later!"

Outside, the Bronx was alive with Jamaicans selling incense and bootleg copies of recent movies and drug dealers huddled in front of brightly lit bodegas looking out for any signs of "Maggie." Teenage banjee girls with door-knocker earrings and baby strollers cruised Fordham Road as we strolled toward 169th Street in search of Sal's dealer, T-Boogie. Another stop for Crazy Horse. We spilled some on the floor to feed the "*muertos*" before hunting the Bronx for any signs of him.

Walking the streets like we owned them, we were clueless to the fact that we looked like undercover cops. All the drug dealers were clocking us. It didn't help that Sal was white; Chris *looked* white, being a light-skinned Puerto Rican raised in a town appropriately named Whitestone, and I was dressed like a white boy with my Stussy T-shirt, expensive sneakers, and Diesel knapsack.

We weren't exactly featuring the latest ghetto gear, and before long we noticed the dealers signaling each other with secret whistles. It seemed no one we stopped had ever ever heard of a guy named T-Boogie.

After walking miles and miles of bodegas and *cuchifritos,* we finally heard a "Yo, Kev!" Simultaneously turning around, we came face to face with a piece of banjee heaven, or maybe just a "piece." There was T-Boogie in the flesh, calling Sal over, a bestial-looking rotweiller at his side.

"T-Boogie! Thank God! We been lookin' all ovah for you! Was goin' on, Ms. Thing? Does your dog bite? What's huh name?"

"Bambi!" he said, snickering. "And I am not 'Ms. Thing' and it's a 'he'!" With T-Boogie staring Chris and me up and down with the most threatening look, and Bambi staring at us like *arroz con pollo,* Sal cleared the air with, "Don't worry about them, papi! They're not 'Maggie'!" Raising one eyebrow knowingly, he snapped his fingers and blew up our spot, "They're 'Angie'!"

Soon the acid really kicked in and the rest was all a blur. Somehow we ended up on some Doña Consuelo's plastic-covered couch listening to a Spanish radio station while a strange woman cooked up a storm in the kitchen. Chris was in tears, tripping hard, haunted by the flying monkeys now hiding behind the many picture frames and dust-collectors decorating the living room. Sal joyfully played around with Bambi in the dining room as if Bambi were a Chihuahua.

A fat old Dominican, drunk off his ass, dressed like he had just stepped off the boat, introduced himself as Don Juan before making himself comfortable in the chair opposite us. Curiously sizing us up, probably thinking we were undercover cops like everyone else, he raised a furious brow, exposing a blistered red eye.

"So! Where chu from?" I knew there was more to his question; maybe he himself was an undercover cop, or maybe he was with the FBI, and Sal wasn't really Sal, and this was all set up to bust me for selling drugs in the clubs. I stared back at him with great intent as Chris answered the question, his eyes focused on the furry monkey tails trying to conceal themselves behind the family photos.

"Puerto Rico!" he answered, gagging at the sight of the roach crawling behind the old man's shoulder. This was no regular roach. It was a *huge* roach, probably able to pick up and smoke its own roach. It had antennae long enough to pick up radio airwaves and MTV, so most likely it was some sort of recording device. I'd seen something like this in the movies.

"PUERTO RICO?" Don Juan cried, jumping out of his skin.

"Why...why...chu look Italian and" (motioning to me) "*chu*...chu look Mexican!"

"Mi mama's from Cagúe, and he's half Ecuadorian!" The roach was now crawling down Don Juan's *guayabera*.

"Oh!...oh!" the old man said, feigning belief; "Cagúe, huh?" Suddenly, the air seemed tense. For a minute, I thought he was going to kill us but instead he noticed the roach and quickly brushed it onto the sticky floor where he crushed it underneath his *chanclas*.

"Chu know, we good famlee, an' we no like NOBODY tearin' da famlee apaht!" he grimly stated, raising his foot to show us the remains of a trespassing soul. Nothing left but flaky armor and white pus. Chris and I nodded stupidly, dimly aware that we were in T-Boogie's apartment, and that Don Juan was making sure we weren't undercover cops sent to arrest his drug-dealing son.

"I likey chu shirt!" *el viejo* said, smiling sarcastically, revealing a slew of missing teeth.

"Thank chu!...I mean, thank you!" I stuttered nervously, studying the multitude of Santeria statues and mini-altars throughout. Suddenly, I was transported to a vast desert having a tea party with Oyá, Yemaya, and Oshún, motorcycles speeding by.

"Where chu get it?" asked the old man, rudely interrupting my dream sequence.

"Que adonde lo comprastes?" he asked, testing my Spanish and trying my patience. I knew what he was up to. Puerto Ricans and Ecuadorians speak very different Spanish, and he was determined to figure out by my accent which influence I had adopted.

"Actually, Chris here bought it for me!" I answered in English, turning to smile lovingly at my papi chulo.

"Ay, papi! You're so romantical!" Chris returned my comment with a sweet kiss on the cheek.

Don Juan's face crumbled.

"Chu? Chu?" waving his crusty finger at us before limping his wrist—the international symbol for homosexuality.

"Uh-huh!" we chimed in, gleaming excitedly. Sal stumbled in, joining us in psychedelic delirium, the room spinning with disco-ball lights and bright colors while Don Juan grabbed his heart and peeled himself off the couch.

"*MARICONES!*" he yelled before heading off toward the kitchen, screaming, "CONSUELO! *ESOS MUCHACHOS EN LA SALA SON MARICONES!*" Consuelo, like any true Latina, wasn't the least bit phased by our homosexuality and shut him up to serve dinner—*pernil con arroz y habichuelas*—while Don Juan went off in Spanish.

After the sixth time the curse "*mama-bichós*" flew from his chapped lips, I got very—"Sal, call Madonna and tell huh to send the limo—NOW!"

"*Mira,* Consuelo! Puhlease pass me the phone so I can call Madonna!" Sal asked, Consuelo taking him seriously.

Next thing I remember, we were outside the building passing around two phat blunts with T-Boogie and some other dogs we didn't even know named Nixon and José. We were sharing them like they were pornos, and we were going to whip out our dicks and jerk off—at least, that's what Sal was praying would happen. The other dogs, they didn't even give a shit that we were faggots, so long as we didn't cross the line and start acting out in public. The other hoods on the block wouldn't be having that, and we'd be sure to get beat, so we were forced to maintain behind shiny sunglasses, looking very Mary J. Blige.

The weed calmed us down a bit, and in complete admiration we watched the little black girls jump rope. Dozing back to the days, remembering how I used to turn out the neighborhood girls with my click-clacks while they desperately tried to keep up with my faggot ass, I began laughing to myself, only to be quieted down with an evil glare from T-Boogie. José was on his cellular with his girl, and all we could hear was a "Yo, baby, *cuando me vas a llevar pa* Macy's?" while Nixon watched me curiously.

"Yo! Can I gets a light?" the neighborhood crack-head, Carlito, bravely approached us to ask.

"Nah! We ain't got none! Go away!" Chris brazenly flaunted the blunt in his face, as T-Boogie, Nixon, and José eyed down Carlito viciously.

"You heard huh, girl! You betta step!" Sal slipped from his butch pose to snap his fingers in the guys' face. Chris and I stood up defensively, backing up our "sista" in case a battle ensued. Confused, Carlito the crack-head walked away totally dissed.

"LET'S FUCK HIM UP!" Chris yelled, feeling all grand, starting to pin back his hair and take off his imaginary high heels to launch an attack.

"*Mierda loco!* No need to get salty, nigga!" Nixon shouted, stopping him.

"Yeah, Xena! Chill out and stop nursin' da blunt!" Jose demanded, snatching it out of his hand with gold-encrusted fingers.

The combination of herb and acid caused a sudden temperature change and next thing I remember, Chris and I were freezing our *nalgas* off in ninety-degree weather while sweat poured down our Ray-Ban shades.

"Wanna go upstairs, papi?" I offered, Chris shivering a "Yes."

"Come on! Let's go upstairs!" I demanded, proceeding to publicly announce that "My boyfriend and I are going back upstairs, because it is too fuckin' cold out hea!"

T-Boogie, Nixon, and José tried to quiet us down before spewing complaints.

"*Coño,* T-Boogie! Why you gotta deal with faggots?" José yelled as we walked away, Sal two steps behind us. However, we only managed two flights before realizing we were completely gone, and we didn't even know where we were or how we got there.

"Are we still at the zoo?" Chris asked. The fear crept up our backs like an army of ants, until a parade of flying monkeys emerged from above to attack us. Sal ran out, eyes glazed, screaming, "HE'S UPON US! THE ANTI-CHRIST IS UPON US! HE'S GONNA KILL US ALL!"

T-Boogie and the others chased after him as Chris and I sat there numb for, like, five whole minutes. Staring into my lover's confused, blood-shot eyes, amidst the madness of our lives, it was in that brief moment that I developed the skeleton of a conscience. With bags of weed at our feet, Chris stared back at me, reaching out to hold me in a tight embrace. With his sweet breath against my ear, I entered the next stage of my high. A single tear ran down my face onto his pale Puerto Rican skin. We held on to each other, clinging to our sanity with wildly enhanced emotion, until the sound of Sal screaming in the distance plunged us into infectious laughter.

Amor Indio: Juan Diego of San Diego

Ramón García

His name was Juan Diego, but his homies called him Indio, 'cause his skin was dark and his cheekbones were high. Knew the streets of East San Diego like he knew the pulse in his heart, had surrendered his life to those streets, to the secret arteries they pumped with dreams and ecstatic visions of escape. Dropped out of school. Had to; too much bullshit to deal with—those stupid *gabacho* teachers couldn't teach him about this thing inside, that pulled him to the streets, to the magic to be found there, to the mysteries that he could not live without. Starting with spray paint in the fifth grade and moving on to pot, speed, coke, and finally junk. He was searching for his own life, cruising down Imperial, looking for the ultimate vision.

Juan Diego had a shiny blue '67 Chevy Impala lowrider. One day he was cruising down Imperial alone, high as an angel holding up the Mother of God. Saw this vision of a girl waiting to cross the street where Imperial intersects 30th. She was waiting for the green "walk" light. That's the meanest-looking *ruca* I've seen in a while, Juan Diego thought. She had the cha-cha hair going in a serious way, sculpted two feet high, white as snow. Juan Diego had no choice but to stop and talk to her. He slammed on the brakes and parked near the curb of the crosswalk. The walk light turned green but she was not going anywhere. It was as if she had been waiting there for him.

Juan Diego could see her up close then. She was radiant, like an angel, but with bigger tits than he imagined angels had. He realized, as he stared at her in astonishment, that the big blond cha-cha hair on top of her head was no cha-cha hair at all—it was a big *Tehuana* headdress, like a giant snowflake framing her face. Suddenly, overcome with fear and desire, he recognized the vision of this *ruca* as the beautiful woman who falls in love with the Indian in the *Cine Millonario* Saturday-night movie. The vision was, in fact, Maria Félix in a *Tehuana* dress from the movie *Tizoc, Amor Indio.* There, in front of him, was that television image of Maria Félix, always playing the grand diva—this time as the romantic painter, fleeing the betrayal of her white lover in Mexico City to find truth in her forbidden love for an Indian, played by Pedro Infante.

She stood by the curb waiting for Indio to say something. Indio looked up at her from the driver's seat, through the rolled-down window. "Ay, mamacita, that's a *chulo* outfit you got on, I swear I saw you on television the other day."

"You did, Ese, it was God speaking to you, telling you of my arrival."

"Whatever you say, *mona*. Want to take a ride?"

"Indio, Ese, I was sent here by God, to be the Queen of your people, to keep them company, to give them glory, to unify them, to be the *Reina* of the barrio."

"How the fuck you know my name, *vata? Hijolé,* how did you get here, man, I don't believe this…?"

"I'm the Mother of God, and God is that television that everyone around here watches with devotion, every single night."

"Ay, I get it, you want to party, well, I know the score, I know where the party's at and I know how to get you there, *chula*."

"I don't want no party from you, Ese. I'm Maria, *La Doña, La Devoradora, La Immortal, La Indomitable*, Maria, *La Unica*, Nuestra Señora de San Diego."

"Whatever you say, *chula* …." Indio felt like he was trapped in a dream, a tripped-out television dream, confusing this *ruca* on the street for the *ruca* in the movie—like in the movie itself, when the Indian Pedro Infante confuses the vision of Maria Félix for a sexy version of La Virgencita. The woman reached into her big JC Penney leather purse and pulled out a white bedsheet. She handed it to Indio. He stood there dumbfounded, confused, not knowing if he should drive away. I must be having a bad trip, he thought.

"Take this and fill it with roses, the color of blood, the color of the blood of your people, the color of memory and genocide." Indio didn't know what she was talking about, this vision in front of him, this vision straight out of Canal 12's *Cine Millonario.*

"*Rosas*—ah, you mean flowers, like the kind that grow on plants and shit?"

"Si, Ese, roses, like the kind Don Emiliano sells by the freeway, go buy everything he's got today and bring them in that bedsheet, here's some money."

She reached into her big leather purse and pulled out forty dollars. He didn't understand, but her beauty touched something deep inside of him and he was compelled to follow her orders. He drove off and a few blocks later he found Don Emiliano, selling his roses by the ramp to I-5 going north. He pulled up right next to him and Don Emiliano asked him what he wanted.

"*Que quieres?*" Don Emiliano asked, irritated because he knew Juan Diego was one of those "*pinche cholos que no sirven pa' nada.*" Don Emiliano had watched Juan Diego grow up, had seen how the years and the intricate delusions of the streets had transformed him into this *loco* with visions in his eyes. The *niño* had it in him, that something that pulls them to the street, that lawlessness that respects nothing, not even its own death. Don Emiliano always knew that Juanito, who had been a *callejero* since he was little, would end up *destrampado, un sin verguenza, un desgraciado.* He didn't know what Indio wanted with him, but he was afraid, because Indio was a "*drogadicto,*" as the people in the neighborhood referred to him in whispery indignation, and *drogadictos* are capable of anything.

"Don Emiliano, Ese, sell me all your flowers, here's forty dollars," said Indio. Through the open window of his lowrider he offered the money. Don Emiliano didn't know what to do; he thought of the evil intentions that Indio could have and catalogued them quickly in his brain.

"*Pa que quieres todas mis flores?*" he asked with suspicion.

"I got to give them to Maria, the *ruca* in the movie Saturday night—you know, the one that has the hots for the Indian *vato* who thinks she's the Virgin Mary. She wants all your flowers, she's waiting for me at the corner, she's *bien guapa,* just like on TV, and I think she's serious, you understand, Don Emiliano, don't you, you were once young, weren't you?"

"Si, *hijo*, I was once young, *pero no destrampado como tú*, I see your mother at church, always lighting candles, praying to *La Virgencita*, I know she worries about you, why don't you talk to *el Padre* Carlos, he's helped boys like you, he can help you."

"Si, Don Emiliano, some other day; today, this *ruca,* Maria, is waiting for me at the corner and I got to get her those flowers, she gave me the money for them." Don Emiliano hesitated but he decided to take the money and give Indio the flowers. He figured if he didn't take the money somebody else would. Better he than another *destrampado*. He handed him the roses, took the money. Indio spread the bedsheet on the passenger seat and bundled the roses inside. Don Emiliano watched, underneath the shadow of the freeway, and thought to himself, We've lost this one too. God, *why*? Why do they do that to themselves?

It was dusk in East San Diego and darkness was descending on the city. The Imperial Boulevard strip was beginning to fill with cruisers and the people of the night. Indio drove back to the crosswalk where he had encountered the vision of Maria, the *ruca* movie-star goddess, and she was still there, posing, as if the headlights from the lowriders cruising by were the flashbulbs of photographers. He pulled up at the curb, like he had done before.

She was smoking in a majestic manner particular to her, divinely illumined by the barrio night lights.

"I got the roses, *chula*, here, they're all yours," he said, handing her the roses, wondering what she would do next.

"Thank you, Indio," she said, taking the bundle in her arms, and then she disappeared in the flash of a lowrider headlight. The bundle of roses in the white bedsheet was on the sidewalk. She was gone, she had disappeared. He was scared. He thought he might have imagined it all. He got out of the car to pick up the bundle of roses. He opened the bundled bedsheet, there, in the middle of the sidewalk, among the lights of the shops and the flashes of headlights. Imprinted on the sheet was the image of Maria, just as she had been in the movie in her most sublime scene, in her most beautiful moment: when she's dressed as a *Tehuana,* at the Indian festival, rebelling against the racist, patriarchal ideas of her bourgeois father. Indio would take the bedsheet to Father Carlos; el padre would understand and know what to do. And so he took it to Father Carlos; walked seven blocks to the church and handed over the sheet with the image. Father Carlos took Indio in his arms and said, "I'm glad you have come to see me, I hear God calling you." Father Carlos could see Indio was sick. Months later Juan Diego would finally answer God's call, after being sick for weeks. It was a fine May morning when Juan Diego's heart stopped forever. His mother, Doña Maria, claims to have seen *La Virgen de Guadalupe* in Juan Diego's eyes in his last moments on earth. Then he shut his eyes as his life raced past him. And when Doña Maria forced them open *La Virgen* was gone from the center of his pupils. Then Juan Diego's mother cried for her dead son, tears she believed were blessed and sanctioned by the *Virgen* herself. As for the bedsheet with the image of Maria Félix as she appeared in *Tizoc, Amor Indio*, el padre knew where it belonged. He donated it to the neighborhood gay bar, a place called Pedro's, where the mistress of ceremonies at the drag shows was a Maria Félix impersonator.

The image was hung by the bar and underneath it a candle was lit every time a person in the neighborhood died of el SIDA. Father Carlos had put a single candle at Maria Félix's feet the day Indio, Juan Diego, died. And now, every time somebody passed away from the disease, Maria, the mistress of ceremonies, would light the candle underneath that glorious image of herself, that image of love and salvation.

Strong Arms

Albert Lujan

Man only plays when in the full
meaning of the word he is a man,
And he is only completely a man when he plays.
—Friedrich von Schiller

At the age of six I declared my love, my desire, my utter need, out loud, to the image on the smooth convex surface of my family's Zenith color television console. From my seat on the tangled shag of the living room I was levitated forward by a force so magnetic that it pulled my tongue from my mouth and my eyes from their sockets, to vibrate only inches from the screen. It pulled the words from my mouth.

"I want you."

I touched the screen and closed my eyes the way I did when choosing a wish before blowing out the candles on birthday cakes.

"I want you soooooo bad."

When I opened my eyes, the object of my desire had vanished, replaced by a "Parkay–Mantequia" debate between a tub of margarine and a monolingual white lady demanding that her butter speak English only.

I vowed to sit there, in front of the television, until I saw again the commercial that so transfixed me; a vow that only lasted till 8:30, my bedtime. I swore I would resume my vigil at dawn. I would see it again. See *him* again. There, I said it. Not out loud, of course, but secretly, with conviction and desire.

Who was he? Why hadn't I heard mention of him in the schoolyard or park? All night I thrashed these questions around, between dreaming and waking. He was on my mind when I woke up. It seemed I'd imagined him, but my dreams were so detailed that I knew, deep down, he was real.

That next morning, before school and between bites of Alpha-Bits cereal, he appeared to me again, on Channel 2.

"Mom, hurry mira lookit, hurry mira lookit! The one I told you about. Hur-ryyy!" I sprayed milk and bits through my nose across the table as I bolted for the TV. Clearly she didn't sense the urgency in my screams. By the time she reached the living room, from the kitchen, where she wrapped a beans-and-rice burrito for my lunch, he was gone.

"Well? Estoy lookit-ing. What? Who?" she asked from the kitchen doorway, where she stood and tried to look interested. Her inability to read my mind or my heart disgusted me. I ignored her. "Next time," I thought, while flipping channels furiously, "you should run to me when I scream. Like I'm expected to when *you* scream." I turned the knob from channel to channel, backward and forward and around and around. He was gone again. Dang.

"Anyway, mijo, it's time for you to go to school. Apaga la TV off," she said.

It was too late to pretend that I felt sick in order to spend the day in front of the TV. A successful sick act had to begin the night before or the minute she woke me up. I'd clutch my pansa and make asco noises. Ditching was for kids who had endless amounts of quarters to drop into pinball games at the liquor store or parents who both worked. I had neither. It was go to school or be forced to stay in bed with no TV and a thermometer stuck in my butt every hour.

Plan B had me rummaging through the medicine chest before breakfast for something that would have the school nurse calling home to let my mother know she was sending me home for the day. I examined the various pills of every color and shape. I resisted eating the Hershey-imitation Ex-Lax. I tried that the day Luke and Laura were scheduled to be married on *General Hospital.* It worked, only I spent the whole day on the toilet and missed it all. I pushed the children's multi vitamins off to the side and selected the bottle with the baby-blue colored pills in it. The label read "Midol." I popped the top and poured three into my pocket. After all, I wasn't suicidal, I was in love.

"I'm talking to you!" Her voice called out, a few octaves deeper. I flipped and flipped.

"Shut the TV off." I turned the knob again. She pulled off one of her pantunflas and smacked me across the back of the neck.

"Now!" She motioned to the door by shaking my brown lunch bag. I stomped across the room, snatched the bag, pushed my way past her and out the door, letting the screen door slam. She hated that. I didn't lean in for her usual good-bye kiss. I felt I was getting too old for that anyway.

On the walk to school I ate the pills from my pocket. I tasted the chalky bitterness and gagged. I silently beckoned to Him. I mouthed His name. Called it out. Even chanted it. Armstrong. Mr. Stretch Armstrong from Hasbro. Hasbro—where was that magical country? I wondered. Strong arms. Yes, clearly he was very strong. Buff like the Tasmanian Devil but in complete control. Stronger than any Tonka truck I'd ever owned and destroyed. He had powerful arms with shoulders out to *there* and legs so muscular it was clear he would never be able to cross them like a girl, even if he wanted to. He had a Bob's Big Boy soft-serve chocolate ice cream flip going on. Sexy, of course, but in a manly way. Painfully blue eyes. He held a sensual half-grin/half-snarl that said, "I'll be your special friend, but don't fuck with me 'cuz I could still kill you with my hands if I have to."

Stretch was quite confident too. Proud of his hard-earned physique. All he ever ran around in was a pair of Speedos. Red. They looked like they were painted on. He was the color of Band-Aids. He reminded me of those masked Mexican wrestlers on Spanish TV. Sin máscara. G.I. Joe and that old sissy, Ken, were obviously ashamed of their scrawny bodies. I was quite disappointed in them, considering how hard it was to get their clothes off.

On the TV commercial, it showed these two little honkey bastards pulling at Stretch's arms. Then along comes another blond demon with his token light-skinned black friend with relaxed JFK hair. And they get to yanking on his legs. And they pulled and pulled as if he were some kind of human pup tent. Like pink taffy. Stretched sadistically to the limit, he then snapped back into shape. I concluded, on my own, that that was why his name was Stretch. But still... "Stop it, you little greedy sons of bitches! Go stretch your little baby sisters or puppies or something. Jesus Christ, just leave my man alone! Can't you understand that those arms were made to wrap around me? To hold me? To cradle me?" And yes, in retrospect and after considerable therapy, to be a surrogate father figure.

At school I couldn't concentrate. I felt kind of lightheaded and kept needing to pee. At my desk I misspelled his name over and over again on my H.R. Puffinstuff notebook. If I got him for Christmas (nine months away) I would never mistreat him. If I got him for my birthday (ten months away) I would cuddle him. Rest him on my chest like some mini-manchild. Feed him mini-muscle bars so that he could have the strength to put Ken in a headlock and make him smell his ripe pits. Scissor-lock G.I. Joe's stubbly face between his powerful legs. "Hold still, recruit. That poor excuse for a beard is gonna give my crotch razor burn." Stretch would be giving the orders in my playroom: "Ken, you little nalga face, rub my feet."

At lunchtime, after I threw away my burrito, I stood in line in the cafeteria holding my bile-yellow fiberglass tray loaded with bile-yellow food. The guy in front of me, this gangly third grader, kept reaching around, checking the contents of his book bag with one hand and trying to balance the tray with the other. It was as if he were afraid some bully was gonna steal his math book or something. Or someone. I saw it. From the edge of the book bag flap I saw it protruding like some obscene, pink udder. Like an arm. A strong arm.

Oh my God. That spoiled little mocoso son of a bitch had my Stretch Armstrong in his backpack. Only one day after the commercial aired for the first time. How hard did he have to whine to get him so soon? And he had the nerve to bring Stretch to school with him. Nine months 'til Christmas, ten 'til my birthday. It just wasn't fair. There he was, mi amor, sequestered between a Pee Chee folder and a *Mad* magazine. My vision was blurring and I tried to look away.

By the time we reached the milk I was hyperventilating. I was so enraged and jealous that I started gagging. Everyone around me was going "eeiiuu" and moving away. I instantly reacted. I jerked forward, snatched Stretch from the backpack, dropped him onto my tray, pulled my tray to my chest, and spilled creamed-corn and fruit cocktail on myself. Still I held him tight next to my thumping heart and obscured him. I was delirious and a little nauseous. The little punk let out a scream.

The Lord works in mysterious ways, 'cuz all of a sudden projectile vomit sprayed from my smiling face. I was wild. Kids ran in all directions. Like a far-reaching sprinkler, I caught most of them on their pants legs. Everyone screamed. It was pandemonium. They cleared out a wide-open get-away path and I took it, laughing, gurgling, almost drowning in my barf, clutching the tray to my chest. I was halfway out the cafeteria before I heard the third grader scream, "Hey, puke-boy's got my doll!"

Doll? Is that all he thought Stretch was? Some toy to stuff into a chest like some old deflated Hoppity-Hop? I thought not. He really didn't deserve him. I ducked into the teachers' restroom. The ladies'. Jumped into a stall. "Oh, Stretch," I murmured. I licked the food off his hairless, cool, smooth, supple, pink body. Sucked clean his face that revealed eyes more heavenly than I'd imagined. His body was fleshy, heavy, and squishy and smelled enticingly of new shower curtains.

"Oh, Stretch, I love you." He was the first man I'd ever kissed with such abandon. Such desire. "But they're coming for us. They'll want to take you from me." There was nowhere to hide him. He didn't fit in my pockets. I tried to stuff him into my pants and that was kinda nice but really obvious. I could hear them outside. They had followed the trail of puke and food. "You're mine, Stretch, forever. No matter what," I vowed.

I pulled the packet that contained the napkin, straw, and 'spork' that had stuck to my shirt. "Before they take you from me, my love, we must take the blood oath." Yes, I was a bit melodramatic for six years old. My favorite after-school pastime was watching the tail end of *Ryan's Hope,* all of *General Hospital,* and, in the evenings, telenovelas with names like *Anamaria Del Callejon.* I slashed the back of my hand with the spork, but getting through Stretch's skin was a little harder. I jabbed him, bit him like a rabid dog. Pulled at him 'til his rubberband-like veins loosened a couple of my teeth. Nothing. It took a couple of hard jabs with my pencil to finally puncture the tough hide on his arm.

I put my bleeding hand to his face. "Drink, lover." I held him over my face and squeezed out his pink, gummy insides, which dangled sensuously and thick like melted mozzarella. I put my mouth over his whole arm and sucked it. I sucked it like it was an Otter Pop. Like it was my thumb. Like a mother's tit. And yes, I sucked his arm like it was a pinga. Okay? I sucked his insides into me. It tasted like Ponds cold cream and paste. I squeezed his chest. I wanted to devour that man. Keep him with me. Inside of me. Give birth to him later. Tears ran down my face. I milked him 'til he was just a shell of a man. I sucked until I passed out under the Kotex dispenser.

I woke up in the hospital. His nontoxic goop lined my insides and blocked my air passage. A 125-year-old nurse told me that I had turned blue, "…just like a Smurf." I had to have my stomach pumped. A tube stuck in through my nose and down into my stomach to feed me beige fluids for two days. Every morning and every evening, a sudsy enema.

At the hospital my parents, and some relatives whom I only saw on Easter and Christmas, watched me nervously, praying the rosary over me and pulling my arm with the I.V. in it to make the sign of the cross. They lavished on me welcomed kisses, Spanish comic books I couldn't figure out, and a Lite-Brite set with a note taped to the top of it that read, "Do *not* swallow the pegs! They are *not* JUJU-BEES!" I had a strange feeling that from then on everybody would be watching what I ate very closely.

That night I fell asleep with the soft, colorfully glowing Lite-Brite set clutched to my chest. On it was the first message I wrote. My first love letter: "I ♥ S.A. 4-ever."

Guerrillas

Daddy

Ricardo A. Bracho

one.

I no longer have a father—and I am one.

It is here, in this chasm of fatherlessness, where I must construct a definition of love. It is not easy, this business of fathering, of loving and of loss. I lose myself so easily in my lack of answers, the places in my body where I cannot find my father, those endless aching spots where I do not respond to being called papi. Fanon says, "O my body, make of me always a man who questions."

But the man who gave me Fanon to read as a child is no longer here for me to quest with. My grief is as fresh as the rich sod under which my father was not buried but where I imagine him now lying. And then there is this child I could have never imagined, who calls me papi, whom I call nigga miss thing mi rey my baby baby sweet baby, as I call him to join in the world laid before him—nationalist n communist, ghetto n elite, comadres n compadres of multiple crisscrossed genders n racializations. A world where the norm is butchmamis n fanciful fathers, where a woman, a feminist, una mujer mexicana y lésbica, knows she has done good work when her son doesn't ask her until he's five, "what's a husband, mami?"

My baby wants me to have a boyfriend. He picks em out for me when I take him down mission street. He always be picking out soot-faced brothers; usually, if not begging, they're criminals and he asks them and me, "is that your friend?" I don't have money to give my child, nor land nor entitlement. All I got is the knowledge of this body we share and a sense of streets like n different from this one. But babyboy got the right questions. "Is that your friend?" Are these connections possible? Or do we got to watch our backs? My boy know the names of 3 buses home, his address too, cuz you got to be able to walk down the street by yourself and get your ass home.

two.

My father died when he was 58, I was 26. Until then I would sleep in his bed with him, kiss him hello n goodbye or just for emphasis, walk shoulder wedged into sobaco n arm thrown over each other down the street. He was/is an impossible man. Belligerent and headstrong and full of corazón y coraje and bewildered by this foreign country and acute in his analysis of its fatal distortions. He was a small man, shorter even than short me, but huge in his joy and rage. A working-class chilango marxist, a barrio-dwelling doctor who could actually be called a community healer, a person many adopted as father, a man who came into his prime as a grandfather. A gift I would have liked to have given to my son, but they never met and I am so unsure if what he left within me can shine through. I am, after all, a small, impossible man who now has no strong arm to wedge my shoulder in. A daddy's girl who has the misfortune to become a man without male elders. I have aids n cancer n cointelpro n angel dust n the lapd n our own hand on the trigger to thank for that. My short life is landmined with cemeteries. This essay could be made up solely of the black n brown names of all my murdered n still be just as long. My father taught me the meaning of the word genocide at a very young age. I have spent my short life watching this word expand and swallow so many I call mine. And always, even in the frenzied infancy of my homosexuality, I knew I wanted to be a father. I just never knew I would become an orphan.

three.

I wonder what kind of sense of race my son will arrive at, given the many migrations made between Mexican/American by his mother's and my peoples. Hispanic, urban indian, narrow nationalist, multi-culti bay area-ness. They're all available even if they all make me wince. I am not a believer in biology or other forms of western romance.

four.

My child thinks me odd. One night while bathing him and watching his brown body turn the clear water black he explains that he is brown and that I am red and black (which my friend the theorist and novelist reid gómez says is an accurate reading of my cultural politics and of course I think of elegua) and that while I am a papi I'm not like other papis cuz I'm more like his (maternal) grandmother than his grandfather. He calls me mister and I call him sister, the name I once used over instant coffee with my mother, not dead now just insane and newly dedicated to that blond baby jesus. And I called my daddy daddy or my old man and for almost the entirety of my 17th year I called him nothing else but asshole. I was/am an incredibly willful exasperating obnoxiously articulate n cultured child. My father always said he regretted when I learned the word no. I don't always listen to my son's no. But I am trying.

I don't want to be a perfect parent, the model postfeminist sperm donor or the Chicano neopatriarch. I don't want to be a soccer coach or even necessarily keep the boy outta trouble. I of course want him to survive, and know that this is not easy. And here I hear Jaime (Cortez, our intrepid editrix) asking me, do I mean "thrive?" A life better than the crackheads outside his alley-facing front door? And I can't say I want that mad drama for this child, but I want to help build the boy strong enough so he can survive even that.

Standing outside the opening night of my first play, I and my brother are as flossy n suited as we want to be and 24th street can take. Amid the blunts n bumps n love we just marvel at the blessing that we aint dead. I make this prayer, looking into my beloved bro's m&m brown eyes: I want to live for my son, maybe a bit longer than our father got to live in our lives.

five.

I did not find my father erotic as a child. I had three other loves: my very moreno muy chicano vecino, 2 years older but so much more boyer and normal than me. He's a chp now. The quarter-breed neighbor being raised by his abuela tejana across the street n my dad's compadre, an afro-*panameño* with a thirst for revolución, ron n pretty pretty girls. But since his death I have rediscovered my father in my sex, in my pleasure in both my force n vulnerability. Oh daddy, when I am naked, I know I am somehow nearer to you.

My child finds me terribly erotic, as he does nearly every adult body he has access to. A baby all up in people's booties who is now learning his and other's limits and delights in saying he needs privacy to dress and pee. But he still peels up my shirt and squeals at the hair that lines my pansa y pecho. He assures me he will never have any, as he is also sure that his mother will never age, batman is indestructible, and that if he closes his eyes he is invisible. As sure as I was as a child that the revolution was coming, that we weren't going to stay in this fucked up country, and that I would not inherit my papi's tangled black cross of hair that covered him from belly to breast.

six.

The last thing I did for my father while he was still awake, conscious, n mobile, before his bone marrow transplant went wrong n he spent his last few horrible days on life support while his 4 boys and one princess of a girlchild fought bitterly with his new wife and with the complete shock of the fact of his death … the last thing I did for him was bathe him. He could not speak because the preparatory chemotherapy had closed his vocal chords, n his head was badly shaved. But my father was a neat clean-smelling man, so bathed n shaved he would be. I washed him and he was so small so shrunken so almost already gone. I choked back the knowledge that this was it, the last time. I made love to him with soap n water n sponge n called up my orishas n our egun through the drain n echo of this cold yanqui institution where my father would die. I returned him to his bed n he waved me out n I knew our relationship was complete. Not perfect nor uncomplicated nor not fucked up but full of my body n his body n how they signify in the discontinuities of our separate n shared histories. This is what I have to give you, son. This sense of daddy.

seven.

My man did not make it to my baby's birthday. Well, it's more complicated than that. He's not my man. He calls it an intimate friendship. Or he did until he found himself lost in the eastoakland hills for an hour and a half n then suddenly found himself in his own father's abandoning body, the one who never made it to his birthdays, so he went home n hurt n didn't call for another day and a half. I worked my ass off for this party, spent all the money I had n then some of my friends', n rolled 132 enchiladas that my trucho homies made from scratch and bought my son a ridiculously expensive cake, all fresh cream n white cake with summer berries to approximate his want for a cherry pie cake n a red power ranger piñata that he himself split in two n that poured out chocolate kisses n special darks n not no cacahuates n nasty-assed mexican candy. I assembled niggas I believe in, what I know to call beauty, the brilliance that is this diasporic debris. But the man I call papa never arrived. Papa, the same name I use to call my son to me n they are, to this date, the only males I have been able to share a bed with since my father died. I avoided my son the whole day cuz I didn't want to have him ask me, as everyone else did, where my man who is not my man was. Cuz my son love him, knows his phone number, chants his name, and calls him his own. It helps that this blackitalian man is a grown up dead ringer for my boy's blackcuban whitebelgian bestfriend. N it hurt so much cuz I love birthdays more than any holiday n my son is a crab boy like me n there aint nothing like summer birthday parties n I had perfect ones with tons of folks n fresh horchata n jello mexican style with sweetened condensed milk n knox. My daddy hated the hyper-capitalism of christmas and was forever forgetting our ages but I had the best birthdays of anyone I know. So much so that I am writing a play, what my wife-compadre-mission-indian-mexican-all-around-youth-arts-activist yvette gómez calls an autobiographical fairy tale, to pay honor n heal my broken into a thousand piñata parts manless and fatherless heart.

And it is with this same busted candy heart that I hear from the man who is never to be my man, but whose brilliance and beauty will ever mark me, that it was just too much for him—me and the matter of this child and this raucous crew I call family. I hear my heart crack again but also release a laugh cuz if he thinks this is too much, he shoulda met my daddy.

eight.

One day I will get the tattoo on my right inner thigh. Daddy in cholo cursive, the baroque stem of the D bordered by my father's birthdate and his deathdate floating next to the afterflourish of the

y. Above will be my birthdate and it will all be underlined by 1993, the year that saw my son's premature arrival in this embodiment of land, spirit and desire; genders, nations and histories.

To and through the man I called daddy and the boy who calls me papi, for and with Gabriel Morales, Veronica Majano, Wura-Natasha Ogunji and Mr. Jhay G.W. Green.

The Last Stand of Mr. America

Jason Flores Williams

My prayer to Lord High Jehovah Yahweh: "Lord, allow for Lady California to be in her room. And if she is, give me the courage to stand against society and fuck her in the ass." That's right, I'm asking god for the courage to fuck a man in the ass. In my defense, however, I accuse god of making a grievous error in allowing Lady California to be born as a man. I therefore amend my prayer to god, and say: "Lord, you fucked up in making Lady California a man. Allow me to put things right and fuck her like a woman. Amen."

I come to the door; she's there. A dark angel staring in the mirror. The innocent Narcissus of Rockets and Missiles—the cavernous sex club of my addiction. The dark place where trannies, queers, and heteros scream out in disjointed unity. Tonight she wears a long, flowing, black dress, adorned with fringe that dances over her body like imps and demons. She wears black lipstick and a red rosary around her neck. She is the Virgin Mary on heroin. A walking requiem for my heterosexuality.

She senses me almost immediately, glances over, and waves me in. As though in a dream, I step into her room. Without saying a word, she points to a chair in the corner. I sit. She closes the door to our tomb, and then takes a seat on the floor across from me. I feel like an eighth grader about to be laid for the first time. My cock is erect. My mind is entangled. I can't conceive of this person as anything other than beautiful woman—a dangerous state of affairs.

In lilting alto, she says, "I was hoping you would come by tonight." Nervous, but feeling very sexy myself, I respond, "I was hoping you'd be here." We soak each other in. There is strong chemistry between us. I think of marriage, then quickly quash the thought. I say to myself, "This chick has a dick this chick has a dick," but it doesn't resonate. I'm out on the perimeter. There are no rules for this. All I see is a person to whom I'm fatally attracted. I pull out the Jamesons and take a long, stabilizing pull. I hold out the bottle.

She takes a good swig then hands back the bottle. "What do you like to do, Sam?"

"I like to do a lot of things," I say, trying to sound sexy. "What kind of things do you like to do?"

"Whatever it is you want me to do."

The world is here. I am in the driver's seat. The only thing standing between me and real sexual pleasure are the morals and mores that have been kicking my ass for twenty-nine years. I could fuck her a million different ways. What will it cost me, though? Will I be able to come back?

My subconscious belches up weird memories that I guess are meant to be answers, but are really no clearer than fucking Zen koans. Me and the gang, around seven or eight years old, hanging out in a big ditch with our bikes. Summertime. At the end of this concrete ditch is a pile of dirt, maybe three or four feet high, with a thick board for a ramp. We debated for hours: Could it be done? Was it certain death? Who had the courage to attempt such a feat?

Toward nightfall and the clock is ticking, soon everyone will have to go home for dinner. I am one of the leaders of our gang of about ten little dudes. In these dare situations it was always either me or my best pal, Dave "The Dog" McGruder. He was a good guy, excellent athlete, but he fucked up and got a girl pregnant and married her in his senior year of high school. I have no idea where he is now.

The Dog wasn't going to do it. It was me or nobody. Without saying a word I hopped on my bike. The gang went wild, screaming and running after me as I raced furiously toward the hill. Coming closer, coming closer. Should I pull out? Never! Baboosh!

The next thing I remember is waking up in the hospital. I had a concussion, broke my jaw, and fractured my kneecap. The board had given way the minute I got to it. Cracked right in half. I ended up flying head-first into a stack of cinder blocks. Looking back, I can say that it was 100 percent worth it. I was from that point on a legend. Untouchable. In the Hall of Kid Fame.

If my old pals could see me now, they wouldn't be so stoked. The legend of Villanova Street on the verge of going fag. Jesus Christ, how did I get into this situation? Aren't I supposed to be married by now? Where are my 2.4 kids? Where's my safe house in the suburbs? I am pathologically attracted to a man in women's clothes, but what an amazing manwoman she is.

"You like to suck it?" I ask.

She opens her mouth and sticks out a long, skinny tongue. "I'd love to suck you, Sam." And moves toward me.

The time is now. Do or die. If I don't move, I'm going to be sucked off by a transvestite. It will undoubtedly be the greatest blow job of my life from what amounts to the hottest woman I have ever been with. There are no answers, only instincts. Lady California sits next to me and puts her hand on my upper thigh. Her beautiful head is on my shoulder. I am harder than I have ever been. She rubs lightly. She is treating me gently, seducing me. My heart palpitates. I ask myself who I am, but the question has no meaning. There is only the silence between Lady California and me. Her hand goes up my thigh, almost at the crotch. Her fingernails are painted black to match her lipstick. A weird subconscious koan belches up again and I am suddenly reminded of James Brown.

Not the singer James Brown, but my friend James Brown. He is the only black friend I ever had. We went to college in New York together. He was incredibly sharp, but with a lot of psychological problems stemming from the issues that a black man in this society has to deal with. I had a couple of chips on my shoulder at the time as well, so we got along famously. We used to get drunk at his apartment in Harlem and then go off into the city looking for trouble. We pulled all sorts of capers: we'd go up to the roof and drop water balloons on crack dealers, we'd break into Rockefeller Center and piss on the ice rink, we'd throw stink bombs into hip bars in the West Village. It all, somehow, made moralistic sense. The world was our enemy, and it felt right.

We hatched a plan to break into a synagogue, steal the Torah, and then deliver it to a tenement where we knew skinheads were squatting. We made it to the synagogue, but by the time we got there we were too drunk. We ended up breaking down a door, tripping an alarm, then passing out in the temple, only to be awakened at gunpoint by New York's Finest. They arrested us, and we spent the night in jail. Being good college boys, we got off with probation and community service.

James was more shitfaced that night then I'd ever seen him. He was out of control: causing scenes, yelling at the cops, whipping his dick out, picking fights. The cops came to isolate him, but James wasn't going down without a fight. It took three cops to handcuff him and move him out. It was a thing of defiant beauty. What I remember, what flashes in my mind like a red neon sign, is what James yelled to me before they took him away.

"Tell 'em!" he screamed furiously. "Tell 'em what it is! Tell 'em!"

I wish it weren't so clear to me now, but I know exactly what he meant.

"Be a man," he was saying. "Be your own man. Don't let these fuckheads take you down."

I have failed James in many ways. More important, I have failed myself. I am not proud of who I am, and I have most certainly let the fuckheads take me down. I don't know what it exactly is that Lady California represents in my life, but I know it's something important. For once, I need to know that what I'm doing is pure.

She's massaging my crotch. I gently take her hand and stare into her eyes. "I need some time to think about this. I hope you don't mind?"

"I understand, Sam. I'll be here."

With love in my heart I quickly get up, knowing that if I hesitate I will lose my resolve and remain with her. I kiss her hand and say, "We'll talk later." I move to help her up but she refuses, wanting to remain on the floor.

"I need to cool down," she says with a wry smile.

"So do I." And exit.

Upstairs there isn't much of a scene, only a few old fags talking on the bed. I feel lost but strong, like a sturdy boat caught in a storm. There's a moment in the movie *Pale Rider* where one of the men, when discussing whether he should make a stand with the others against the outlaws, says, "I am not a brave man, but I ain't no coward neither." The same goes for me. I am not a man of integrity, but I am not a jellyfish either. Lady California is a chance to be decent. I wish I had someone I could discuss it with.

I don't have any friends anymore, really. Friendships made in adulthood are all conditional. They are based on jobs, playing golf, getting drunk. They don't transcend category. What can I do? Invite a pal out for drinks after work, then ask him what he thinks about my getting a blow job from a transvestite named Lady California? Absolutely out of the question.

I pass by the sadomasochism chamber (where there is again no action) and move into the lobby with the big sadomasochistic wheel of fortune. A skinny queer is eyeing it hungrily but cautiously. I know just where he's coming from. I enter the juice bar.

I am welcomed immediately and enthusiastically. "Sam, it's good to see you. Have a seat." Music to my ears. In my confusion I've managed to come to the right, friendly place.

"Miss Nowhere, the pleasure is all mine," I say. I sit down at my old stool. At the other end of this tiny bar is another fellow—an old school queen dressed in a boa. He has the look of a gay-world elder statesman. Definitely aged, but not frail. I can already tell that he's charming.

"Sam," says Miss Nowhere, "meet Quentin."

Quentin immediately holds out his hand and says, "Always a pleasure to meet a fellow Scorpio."

Surprised, I shake his hand. "How did you know?"

Gallantly, "We wear it like a coat of arms," he says. "Ha-ha."

I decide immediately that I like him. I turn to Miss Nowhere. Before I can say a word, she says, "So what's it going to be tonight, Sam?"

There's not much of a choice. "Coffee, black," I say.

She leans forward and whispers, "Why don't I give you a coffee cup for your whiskey?"

Quentin holds up his dark coffee cup to show that he's already in on the secret. He pulls back his gray sport coat to reveal a bottle of vodka. A Scorpio, indeed.

She puts a red coffee cup in front of me, and I pour the rest of my whiskey into it. The deed accomplished, I put the bottle back into my dark blue sports coat and settle in.

"So how are things in the land of the living?" I ask Miss Nowhere. I feel expansive. No reason to screw around. I sip at the Jamesons.

"I'm doing well," says Miss Nowhere with a philosophical air. "Present company excepted, Quentin and I were discussing how there seems to be lack of real men around these days."

"Of real gentlemen," Quentin corrects graciously. "That there is a dearth of the qualities that constitute the gentlemen."

They've got my interest. "Quentin," I say, "what is it to be a gentleman in today's society?"

He is a distinguished old geezer. A queer to the core. He doesn't talk, he conversationalizes. And we are now on a subject.

"The latter portion of your query, Sam, and by saying this I intend no disrespect..."

I nod my head reverently, indicating that I am fully aware of the laws of intelligent conversation.

"...is arguable. For some would say that to be a gentleman is to be a gentleman in any age. For my part, I am yet to decide on the matter."

Miss Nowhere is in a more assertive mood than when I first met her. "I've decided," she says adamantly, "that it doesn't matter if it's now or a hundred years ago, a gentleman is a gentleman."

"I disagree," I say. I could use a good discourse. "Each age has its own social requirements. Our time is especially complex. Therefore, it might require more to be a gentleman than it used to."

Quentin claps his hands together. "Ha-ha," he says. "Your point is well taken, Sam." He turns to Miss Nowhere and asks, "What do you think of Sam's point? Isn't it marvelous to have with us such an astute and handsome young man?"

I can't help but blush. Quentin is like the grandmother I never had.

"He sure is handsome," says Miss Nowhere. "Only I don't think that I agree."

"And why not?" asks Quentin, thrilled to be moderator.

Miss Nowhere looks very nice tonight. She's wearing a brown angora sweater and a dark, full-length skirt. Sexy, but understated. She leans on the bar a contemplative look comes over her soft face. "Being a gentlemen isn't about wearing nice clothes and opening doors for people. Being a gentlemen is about believing in what's good and standing up for it when the time comes. A gentlemen has beliefs and convictions. He has a sense of justice and fairness. He gives all people a chance."

Miss Nowhere brushes her dark hair out of her face and continues, "Justice and fairness don't change. They've been here since the beginning and will be here as long as we are. The man who stands on the side of justice now is the same as the man who stood on the side of justice a thousand years ago. The only thing that changes are the clothes."

"And thank god for that," says Quentin. "Otherwise justice would be a rather smelly affair, wouldn't it?'

We all laugh and enjoy each other's company.

After a moment and a couple sips of Jamesons, I speak up. "I don't disagree with you, Miss Nowhere, but I can't help but think that things are a more complex today than they were in the past. Things were more physical back then. Life was based on killing and eating, on survival. If some warlord came into your hut and started raping your wife, you either stood tall and defended her or ran for the hills. Nowadays, it's not so cut-and-dried. Any monkey can help grandma across the street, but who can take a stand against an oil company? We're all caught up in this big net, and no matter how we act it makes us all guilty. To me, being a gentlemen is all about pomp and circumstance. Smile, laugh when you're supposed to laugh, treat people kindly, don't fart in public. All the while we're driving around in a car using gas from an oil company that murders decent people in Kenya. There's no way out. Our tax dollars support wars in Central America where women are raped and children executed." I sip at my Jamesons, not knowing if I had made sense or not.

Quentin, loving a politically charged conversation, says, "Well stated, Sam. But I'm afraid that you're somewhat of a defeatist. On your account we might as well all give in to our animal natures and commence in evil debauchery. Not a bad idea, on the whole," he says with a wink, "but it could turn a bit distasteful, don't you think?"

I raise my cup to him. "Stated like a gentleman," I say.

He raises his cup of vodka in elegant acceptance.

Miss Nowhere pours herself a cup of coffee. "Justice is justice, Sam," she says. "It takes place on a personal level. If you think driving a car is bad, then you shouldn't drive a car. The same goes with eating meat. If it bothers you, don't do it. It all comes down to a matter of personal conscience."

Quentin cogitates. I wouldn't be surprised to find out that he was once a professor. He has an academic quality. "Both of you have stated your positions so eloquently that I don't know which side to choose. At the outset, I was somewhat of the mind that, if I may brutalize Ms. Stein, a gentleman is a gentleman is a gentleman. Notions of justice and fair play are constant ones. They've been at our side in the same recognizable form insofar as, whenever we have outdone ourselves, we have fulfilled," Quentin says, waving his fingers to make quotation marks, "'the better angels of our nature'."

Quentin sips more vodka from his coffee cup. He puts it down and continues. "On the other hand, with the rise of technology, life has become an odd synthesis of the complex and the superficial. One doesn't know exactly where one stands anymore. Thus, in reference to what you said, Sam: Helping a grandmother cross the street just doesn't seem to cut the mustard anymore, does it?"

I shake my head in agreement. I sip my whiskey. I listen.

"Finally, to answer your question," he continues, "it seems to me that the gentleman of today is close kin to the gentleman of a thousand years past. Yet, there is a difference. The gentleman of today must be discerning in his employment of the notions of justice, goodness, and fairness. In other words, Sam, pick your battles wisely."

Have I misrepresented myself? I feel like a liar, but I haven't lied. He is talking to the wrong guy—overrating me on a massive scale. I am the one who watches TV while a woman gets beaten. I'm no warrior battling evil in the world. For that matter, I probably am part of the evil in the world. Humanity is a fucking farce. Life is way overrated. The only thing that keeps me around is the possibility that I might one day end up in an orgy with six supermodels.

"I don't know about that, Quentin," I respond, speaking in couched terms; I don't want him to think me a total piece of shit. "There aren't any clear-cut battles anymore. You stick your head out and it's more likely to get cut off than anything else. I know I must sound jaded, but in a world without meaning, it doesn't matter what you do. So you might as well make yourself as comfortable as possible and hope that the ride doesn't have too many bumps."

Quentin throws up his arms dramatically. "What else is there to say, Sam?" He pauses, slyly. "Other than, 'me-thinks he doth protest too much.' "

A witty, if incorrect, statement. I raise my cup to his erudition. He toasts, as does Miss Nowhere. "I wish it were that way, Quentin. I wish it were." I turn to the barkeeper, saying, "But modern society has a strange way of making people weak, and is definitely ungentlemanly. Things in this world are more confused than ever." I pause, then add, "And I don't care for much in it."

"That's not what I hear," says Miss Nowhere quickly.

I want to deny it, not only to her, but to myself. I can't do it, though. I'm caught. Tonight, when I left Lady California, I didn't know what I was going to do. With every second away from her, though, my resolve has grown stronger. At first I was confident in my ability to leave her tonight without saying another word. Now, I'm like a dry sponge next to a spill: one little push and I'm soaking.

"What have you heard?" I ask.

"All I've heard, Sam, is that she thinks you're an attractive and interesting guy."

"That's all?"

"Not entirely. Girlfriend would kill me for saying...." She pauses intentionally to make sure that I really want it.

"What?" I beg.

"She skipped a big party tonight, just in case you were going to be here."

"Really?" I feel like a schoolboy getting the lowdown on a girl I like. "What should I do?"

Quentin speaks. "Do what your heart tells you, Sam. And if not your heart, then your libido. Ha-ha."

"Easier said then done," I say to Quentin. "I have issues here."

"And you should be thankful, Sam," he says. "A life without issues isn't a life worth living."

I turn to Miss Nowhere. "What do you think I should do?"

This is a serious question for her. She's thinking not only of me, but of Lady California as well. I'm sure that Miss Nowhere has fallen victim to the overactive sex drives of straights such as myself. I am also sure that she couldn't give a damn about my "heterosexual issues." For her, there are no such things as issues—there is simply society.

"You should go talk to her, Sam. She's a human being, just like you. She's waiting for you because there's something in you that touches her."

I sip my Jamesons. "You're right," I say to Miss Nowhere. "I'm going to go talk to her now." I dramatically push my stool back and finish the Jamesons. "Thanks."

"Don't thank me, Sam," says Miss Nowhere. "It's the gentleman in you."

"Yeah, right." I say it to myself as much as to her. I say it to the world and to god and to history and to all humanity. Don't look to me to stick my neck out. I am not above average in any way.

I hold my hand out to Quentin. "Quentin, it's been a real pleasure."

"The pleasure is mutual," he says gracefully.

"Will I be seeing you in these parts again?" I ask.

A wistful smile comes over Quentin's face. "I'm afraid not, good sir. I rarely venture out into the world anymore. I'm much too infirm for this kind of excitement on a regular basis, no matter how enjoyable."

I notice for the first time that Quentin has on a hospital bracelet. There's something beautiful about the fact that he comes here instead of going to a church or an old movie. This is a man who sincerely, devoutly, loves humanity.

I squeeze his hand. "Take care of yourself, Quentin."

"Ha-ha," he shakes back. "Too easy—take care of the world!"

These people are tough.

I tip my head to Miss Nowhere and leave the juice bar for the lobby, where the fag has managed to get himself strapped onto on the big wheel. No one is paying any attention to him. In fact, no one seems to be on the top floor at all. I stare at him for a moment; he stares back. Neither one of us says a word. It is one of the strangest, most awkward silences of my life. He is not upside down, but sideways. I am standing straight up. In gentlemanly homage to Quentin and Miss Nowhere, I step up to the wheel.

As on *The Price Is Right* where they go for the ten grand, I spin. The fag lets out a little yelp and to make sure that he's getting his money's worth, I say, "Spin till you die, you fucking piece of shit. Daddy hates your guts," and give it another good twirl.

A smile comes over his spinning face.

Sun to Sun

Jaime Cortez

Top

Monday, 4:30 a.m. I am the only one left on the raw hilltop of Buena Vista Park. For hours I have wandered these trails in the fog. All about me, the advancing dawn reveals eucalyptus trees receding into gray, soft as Chinese watercolor. I am not so serene. I know what I look like—a desperate carnivore in mid-January, crazy with eating twigs. I can taste my breath, and my clammy jeans are weighted with mist. By now my desperation must be a palpable thing, rusty metal a man could taste on his tongue. I should leave.

Still, I stay.

To the east, past the buildings, across the water, Oakland hides from the thin winter sunlight beneath a dingy blanket of fog. Soon the afterhours clubs will begin belching up speed freaks who will make their way up the trails, frantically extending nightlife into morning. They smell bad, those boys: all night, and sometimes for days, they have sweated out all the shit they pump into their systems. Still, I am grateful when they drop their voluminous jeans and offer up their bony asses.

Yes, I will wait and, perhaps, put my need to rest.

My Buena Vista stories are well known to friends. They have heard tell of the lunatic who stepped out of his pants, dropped to his hands and knees, kissed the ground, and just stayed there for hours, his pale ass prayerfully directed toward the full moon. They know of the night I broke the spell of a three-week sexual jag by reaching under some boy's shirt and brailling the jagged lament inscribed across his torso in KS lesions.

Friends occasionally brave honesty and ask how I can endure such disconnection. Perhaps they think me a cynic, one who has gone through love and come out the other side, damned to mere carnality. They may be right, but I don't think they see how we sex junkies are the last romantics. Ours is the optimism of Mission Street crackheads, scanning the gutters for the perfect rock, that grapefruit-sized orb of contentment that will fix everything forever. Against irrefutable evidence, I believe that around that corner, behind that cluster of bushes, in the putrid back of the bar awaits the perfect sexual encounter, the one that will fill my every void, including those that have yet to hollow themselves out.

My perversity is dear indeed. I wing to heights of optimism and, yes, faith unbearable to others. I endure that Lucifer plunge onto asphalt disappointment several times a month, and still I rise, a proud, terrible creature, popping my hips back into their sockets, spitting out mouthfuls of uprooted molars.

God loved me dearly at some point. I think I believe that my way back is a suspension bridge of flesh.

Coffee

Monday, 7:15 a.m. My drive takes me past the Day Laborer Center, where every morning Mexicanos and their brothers from all points south line up in hopes of finding day jobs in construction, gardening, housepainting, or moving. By seven, a straggly queue winds out the door and down the street. As I approach that corner, I slow my car and roll down the passenger window. I turn left, straying from my route to follow the line of men down the side of the building. They stand in twos and threes, their morning shadows angling up the walls behind them as they cautiously sip from styrofoam cups and chat of the weather and rumored job leads. Their words float through my window on the steam of coffee. I sometimes hear their names. Eliseo. Marcoantonio. José. I hear their Spanish coffee talk. Coffee talk of Guatemala, with its earnest modesty. Coffee talk of Mexico City, with its bombastic rises and deep-coursing irony. Coffee talk of Tijuana, coarse, crude, and peppered with bastard border verbs.

Watchale.

They squeeze my heart in their callused hands, these men. I wish to kiss the furrowed worry from their brows, hold in my hands the secret rounded softness of their bellies. Maybe it's just my curiosity about what a needful man will do for a crisp twenty. Maybe I want to anchor them in place against the riptides of this city. I gaze and drink in their tidy mustaches and dark eyes, their work-worn boots, jeans, and baseball caps—uniforms of readiness.

They hate you here, manito, I want to tell them: your earthen unpreparedness for this coming century of transfigured information shooting across the sky like prayers, your one million baby-bird children and their eternally opened mouths. Your hunger is forever unfashionable. As I drive away, they shrink in my rear view mirror. I turn the corner, and they continue waiting for jobs as the Bedouin wait for rain.

Not Even Net

Monday, 3:30 p.m.

"Fuck outta my way, punk."

"Nigga, I don't wanna have to bitch-slap you, but if I have to, I will."

"Bitch, you wish." This serenade from Clarion Alley wakes me from my party girl afternoon sleep, and I part my curtains to see Amador, Ray, and two other neighborhood Chicanitos shooting hoops. Each point is accompanied by a volley of choice insults.

Their pants droop low about their asses, but still they manage to get in some good play, all the while testing each other.

Pushing. Pushing. Pushing.

Amador goes for a three-point shot. The arc of the ball begins in his ankles and exits through his fingertips, which droop limply in the wake of the shot. The ball drops prettily through the hoop, and his elegantly loose fingers knot into a fist that pumps the air. He plunges his all-elbows-and-knees body right back into the game. The four of them merge and break in vectors of flight and pursuit. They feint and charge and leap and push. Their guardian angels clock in twenty miracles per minute, and at the end of the game no one is hurt. They pass around a two-liter Mountain Dew and disappear it greedily, in the way of boys. Through for the day, they amble past the vomit, piss smells, and amber shards of Olde English bottles to enter the human flow of Mission Street.

Long-necked Amador is not dissimilar in face to da Vinci's Madonna of the Rocks. Every day he walks that milky prettiness past leering prostitutes, ranting crackheads, dismissive girls, scowling gangbangers, and watchful homosexuals. Through Amador, I know something of masculinity. It is far more exquisite and fine than femininity. Women can count on the astounding elasticity they have built into femininity. Only with serious, sustained effort can a woman rupture it. The delicate filigree structure of masculinity, in contrast, splinters at the slightest strain. One wrong move, voice modulation, or clothing choice shatters the brittle machista architecture, and the fuck-up is left standing amid the rubble, vulnerable as a pomegranate in mid-November with its skin ruptured open, tender jewels exposed.

And so, a thousand times a thousand Amadors daily walk sidewalks as precarious as tightropes, while butch dykes and abuelos walk in a line before them, and their hermanitos and babes yet unborn walk behind them, and everyone prays for steady feet and wipes nervous sweat from their upper lip.

Crest

Monday, 10:46 p.m. The taste of loneliness is the taste of toothpaste as I brush before bed on another Monday night. One more week has passed, and my bed remains empty. Surely some colossal failure of connection has occurred that I should be so lonely. Loneliness is a motherfucker and, as Seal noted, a killer. We all know this and will endure much to keep it on the other side of the door. We will hide in our work and manias, bury our faces in the chests of inadequate lovers, or pretend our children need us more than we need them. Most anything is preferable to the crisp reflection in that mirror of loneliness.

As I bathe, I am tender with my body, spreading suds across the fat expanse of my stomach. Dual immersion in bear propaganda and feminist body theory have left me unconvinced that this, my body, is to be loved. Lovable things are, well, *lovable.* When a sex partner ardently grips great fistfuls of my belly and love handles, I am mortified by his appetite. Better that he should admire my face, which I like, or my legs, which are great, but not my obese midsection, my Fred Flintstone toes, hairy shoulders, or unfortunate ass.

Ah well...one liberation at a time, I guess.

Callers

Monday, 11:22 p.m. Abuela visits me from the other side. I enter a room, and she sits at a table in a high-backed chair. Before her, a blue bowl brims with flames. Dipping into it with a leaden spoon, she raises fiery mouthfuls to her lips, inhales them, and swallows painfully, her eyes pulled into squints. Her lashes are all but singed off. Her lips look blistered with burns.

"Do you want some, mijo?" she offers.

"No."

"You get used to it after a while, and then it's not so bad. Especially if you don't make a face and get fussy about the burns.

Really, you should get used to it. It's important." I skim the spoon across the bowl, fill it, and then stop.

"I can't, Abuela."

"Scars are stronger than regular flesh, mijo. More alive. A badge." I raise the spoon again. The ringing of the phone wakes me.

"Can I come over?" Blessed booty-call from an old love.

"Please do." Instant erection.

I fire up the blue light. You arrive in half an hour. Breezy chatter. The familiar quickening. I push your pants past your ass. Shirt over your upraised arms. Press the nude brown warmth of you against the mirror. Relearn your neck with my mouth. No one tastes like you, hijo de puta. The tender ferocity of our rhythms. Cumming is an ecstatic affair, as complicated and impossible as everything else we did together. I hold you for a time and then send you home. You still snore.

After you leave, the slanted light of my lamp reveals a ghost. Your body oils and salts cling still to that mirror. Fickle phantom, visible only in this light, from this angle. This smudge was your belly. These your cock and thigh. Here was your cheek. This is my Shroud of Turin. Proof of great love and torment. I kiss then banish it, wiping and wiping until I see myself clearly in the indigo light. I slip back under covers and luxuriate in the starfish spread of my bare body across the warm expanse of my empty bed.

Nueva Flor de Canela

Pedro Bustos Aguilar

Flor de Canela,
sospiro cuando me acuerdo de ti,
sospiro yo,
sospiro cuando me acuerdo de ti...
no llores más,
ya no sospires,
mira que nunca te olvidaré...
sospiro yo,
sospiro cuando me acuerdo de ti...
—*traditional Purépecha song*

...it was hot that night, hot as hell, hot as Veracruz gets hot in the summer months, and, as we were running out of the car and into the disco, the ol' tunes already audible in the air, I tripped and fell and twisted my ankle, but rushed in nonetheless and started drinking gin-and-tonics and watching the girls.... Fallito Castel came in last, she was the star, she had a long tail on her dress, all that hair, she starts singing and at that same moment it all starts unraveling, it's only the beginning and it's already the end. The wig came off, the eyelashes, the breasts, the color in her face...this is my life, and I don't give a damn for lost emotions, and I was thinking, how do you go from all that glitter to a bare soul in one song? Is it Shirley Bassey that does it for us? No, it's life. It's always only beginning and it's already over every time you think about it. The pain stayed with me throughout that trip, all those days and nights of beer and lust, repressed lust, exuberant lust, but I forgot about it when he fucked me. It was a hotel room, and he was still as beautiful as that day I picked him up in the streets, and the afternoon was for pleasure and I dissed French Composition or I don't know what...the pain of all that makeup wiped with a dirty towel on stage...the pain of my twisted ankle...the pain of my craving, my lust...it's not gone. It just went away in a mental straitjacket of drugs, psychiatric guidance, and self-flagellation; the pain and the urge are back, all coming back to me, and boy am I glad they're here...the pain visited me the other night after the big scare, in the shadows of my old bathhouse, in the shape of that mouth, those nipples, and the cock that I started sucking as if it were all new, all starting again, and I was numb because the pain was back and it felt good to look for an orgasm with the memories of the pain digging into my flesh and staying there, where I am feeling them again and from where they are not leaving anymore, for a while, for now, forever, now I know it, because I'm back to writing, back in front of an empty page, and as I fill it I think of that resilience that made me go into that club and cry inside with Fallito and keep my pain there but forget the pain. My ankle was beginning to swell, but there's always the next gin-and-tonic. Yes, who would have known? There's more of the same to come, all the time, yet it's all newly scary every time, and now I know that I will always keep going back in, back up into the bare soul of the draga throwing away the hair and the self to show the scary other she has inside...that happened to me. But I am not afraid anymore...

En la vieja Valladolid, en el valle de Guayangareo del estado de Michoacán, nació, el 9 de abril del año de 1955, en la Casa de Maternidad "Cuautla" del barrio de la Corregidora, un niño vivo, hijo primogénito de Eva María Clotilde Caballero y José del Carmen Aguilar, vecinos del lugar y unidos en matrimonio, y fue llevado a la pila bautismal a los 15 días del mes de mayo del mismo año en la iglesia de Santa Rosa donde habían recibido el sacramento del matrimonio sus padres y abuelos. Creció entre cunas y rasos, bajo el olor del naranjo y el limón del patio y al amparo amoroso de su abuela materna, el mayor de ocho hijos y el primero de veinticuatro nietos, en los brazos de sus tres jóvenes tías que lo arrullaron en el sigilio de la noche entre campanadas de pueblo viejo y besos robados en las esquinas y las ventanas por enamorados que fueron pasando, y de su mano dio los primeros pasos. Sentado ante el espejo morado de sus tías aprendió a guardar la respiración para no interrumpir los ritos de la vanidad femenina en flor, y aspirando el perfume dulce y pesado de los cajones descubrió el encaje delicado del velo de luto de su abuela, el fino bordado en los guantes negros, las cartas y poemas de un abuelo distante que en la madurez había enamorado y desposado a una casi niña que al momento se volvió una niña vieja. De su mano descubrió el secreto placer de la penitencia piadosa en noches de otoño por la Calzada de Guadalupe, repitiendo los rezos apurados de las mujeres de la Iglesia de San Diego, entre el humo de los cacahuates tostados y los gritos en rima de la lotería de feria, ansiando ganar la clemencia divina y el premio en la tierra prometido por las tablitas de cartón y los granos de maíz. Las madres del convento de la Cruz le dieron bolsitas de papel llenas de esquinas de hostia en anticipo de la Primera Comunión que con sus dos hermanos recibió ahí a los diez años, vestidos de lino crudo y terciopelo rojo que al caerse se rasgó en las canteras del patio de aquella casa del naranjo y el limón, ese día cargados de guirnaldas de flores blancas para cobijar las mesas del desayuno. En el fondo del ropero encontró los zapatos forrados de raso blanco y adornados con ramitos de azahar que guardara de su boda su madre, y se los puso y sintió los tacones clavarse en sus talones y mecer su cuerpo con la gracia de los pasos de sus tías. Caminó esos pasos pretendiendo esa gracia, por las calles y los parques, en las tardes y en las noches, hasta que encontró, a los quince años, el primer beso y las primeras caricias robadas a un extraño, que fue también el primero de muchos en desaparecer, en las sombras del bosque Cuauhtémoc. Después de esperar y buscar, buscar y esperar más, decidió ver el mundo y dejó atrás el pueblo de Valladolid, el valle de Guayangareo, las tardes dormilonas y la tibieza de su abuela, y se fue, y al verlo irse, su madre supo que se iba para no volver.

...but the eyes of the guard stared at me intently as the socks fell on the floor. I was buck naked for a "strip search," and the glare in those eyes gave me back my strength. I remembered I was strong. I train hard to be strong. I sweat and hurt and stretch. And I was, I used to be strong, and at some point my strength left me, and I was helpless. Not anymore, I thought, the next day when I was certain I had survived a night of incarceration, and I knew I was strong. One day I told myself, I am going to be stronger than this virus. And I took a long, long pause to think up a way, until the way came to me, and there I was, at the gym, my first day, still stoned, the last time I've been stoned at the gym, and I haven't stopped since then, except to look at the bitch. And the bitch is coming out fine, except it's scary at times to think how much control I crave over it all, over my body, over my soul, over my mind, over my heart, over my hiv. It took lots of stripping for my strength to come through; back at the detention center was not the first time I've stripped. I stripped before, many times, shedding layers, like a snake, rings actually, and little by little a whole lot of me that seemed like a burden went. This is what happens when you learn to live with your death; your life takes you to places unbethought. So when the eyes of the guard confronted me, naked in that inhospitable little strip room, I started to be less scared for the first time in many years. And I realized that at last the time had come to face all of my fear and weaknesses, and I was just doing it and not thinking anything of it just then, until later, lying down on the bunk, sleepless, then I thought about it, about how I had lived through that, one of my worst fears, and I was still in one piece, and I was not going to crumble, and, when I finally came out of it, out of the fear, of the detention center, of the hands of the law holding me down, I realized I had lifted myself back up, leaving behind the queer femme boy that I was and the transformation, like a drag show, happened all over again in my mind like the latest act in a drawn-out show. I am big now, bigger inside, and I am not afraid anymore. Three years ago I decided I was going to become this, and now I know I have become it, that night in detention I knew I had become it, and ever since I feel the power of my resilience, I feel my strength driving me through it all, I find myself with my feet on the world again. I can use this body that shielded me the night of my fears to look for the evasive pleasure of another body. Even if it is sometimes only from afar, from close afar as they police our desire, with my eyes closed but my thinking open, imagining again the possibility of that body in the bunk underneath getting aroused, the straight man to whom it belongs, eyes betraying loneliness and desire, staring at me, looking into me, and making me feel alive even there in the cell where they have tried to reduce me to less than nothing. I open my eyes cautiously to sneak down into the crotch that his hand keeps caressing, like before, like years back, when other furtive looks gave me the pleasure of a secret lust...

Xalapa verde y frondosa, fría y húmeda, chorreando agua constantemente, lo recibió y lo cuidó, lo sostuvo y lo amamantó. Xalapa lejana y rumorosa lo llenó de libertad y de nostalgia, que era la medida de esa libertad, y allí dio sus primeros pasos lejos de tocadores e hilos de media que se iban, sin el brazo de su abuela rezando por la calzada y sin las manos de sus tías para adornarse el cuello con sus azabaches. Ahí también caminó los pasos de la noche, ahí también buscó, cada vez con más aprehensión, el placer esquivo de los besos y las caricias. Ahí los encontró, Xalapa se los dio por fin, aunque fuera sólo momentáneamente, aunque haya sido sólo para desearlos más y menos encontrarlos después; ahí recibió las lecciones de su educación sentimental que era lo que más que todo buscaba, pues ahí conoció el amor para él imposible pero necesario y necesitado de una mujer madura, una mujer casada que le propuso aprender a amarlo a él vestido de colores brillantes y telas suaves. Ahí también conoció el amor con urgencia de los cuerpos adolescentes que se entregan con ansia, con totalidad, con abandono, con la fuerza de las erecciones mutuas, la seguridad del otro y el desafío de los demás, y entonces supo que seguiría buscando, porque no quería haber ya encontrado sino seguir encontrando más. Xalapa, húmeda y mojada, era como sus baños de vapor de la calle de Allende, en donde la búsqueda seguía cada sábado entre brumas y masajes, caliente por dentro y caliente por encima de la piel. Ahí su mundo de aromas y bilés se transformó en los pasos cadenciosos de las muchachas de la escuela, las bolsas que abrían casi ritualmente para buscar un espejo, una sombra, su reflejo al fumar y tomar café sin el tedio de las clases, en la tibieza de las pláticas de mujeres, con el desdén burlón de los hombres, de lejos. En Xalapa la bella fue también donde una noche, después de haber sido amado y deseado, fue violado por primera vez por aquél sin nombre que lo llevó al baño y lo hizo arrodillarse, lo hizo manosearlo hasta que su pene negro se paró, y doblándolo por la cintura lo penetró sin cariño, con fuerza, y luego le hizo limpiarle la verga flácida. El Alacrán lo rescató de los demás que ya estaban tomando su turno y lo llevó a su casa; de camino, en el parque de los Berros, le dio la mano en la madrugada, lo besó en la boca, y le pidió ir a su casa. El Alacrán le hizo el amor en ese cuarto de estudiante, y ésa fue su primera pasión no correspondida, su primera pasión por encima y por fuera negada. Y después del Alacrán hubo muchos otros, que como él, su deseo anhelaba pero su razón, equivocada, rechazaba.

...fuck when the virus came. I said fuck, it's all over, the endless pursuit, the longing, always looking for the chance that something, someone, will come by and be by me and I'll have my companion and then I'll finally be free of the urging and the needing and the solitude. So when my virus came, fuck, I started this path downward faster and faster, but it was leading me somewhere, somewhere where I'd finally be myself, with myself, at peace; this is the path, fighting this disease, struggling to gain terrain against the ravaging strokes of these creatures I cannot see but certainly feel and know are inside me, wedged right there between my life and my sex, it is here that I am myself, that I come through with full force as I try to understand how it is that self-destruction has turned into love, into the love of me that has eluded me for so long, eluded me from the moment I heard those little scary words, *you came out positive,* which to me meant it's over, your life ends somewhere here, soon, until the moment I could say out loud for me and everyone else to hear, I live with this virus, I have this thing inside me, there are two of us now, until the moment I stopped fighting it out of my life, stopped negating it, and I could finally accept living with it, next to it, within it, protecting it as I have to now because it has become the strongest and the weakest part of me, the place in my life and my body where all the best and the worst are resolved, where the old and the new me meet and are one and as I day by day try to make it the place of harmony, of acceptance, of courage, because I and my virus are imperfection and in the interstices of my flaws and those of these creatures inside lie my life, our coexistence, our best chances to be and be happy, 'cause positive is full of crevices... Is it the virus that took it all away from me when it first entered my body and took over my life? Or was it me, rather, who decided to push it all away, to punish that intruder who was, in the end, now I see, me, part of me, and only me? It was me, it was it, it was both of us looking for a way to be together, queer lovers afraid of taking up a relationship that is bigger than each one anticipated, but the relationship is unavoidable, so here we are together getting through, no longer strange bedfellows, intimate like the inner craving and desire that initially pushed a chemical paradox into the flux of my very core and that turned my outer self into a compromised immune system and my inner self into a gladiator preparing for the next battle with ever-greater weapons, which made me shed my long hair, my girlish face, my silks and satins, and shoot testosterone into the stream of my blood to make the trek to Gold's Gym every day in the winter cold, in the summer fog, in the grayness of my despair, in the joy of my reencounter with the one thing I had going for me since I started out of that dreamy little town of my memories, of my heart, the embracing of a life and a time full of uncertitude, pleasures, and pains that I could only guess, that I keep only finding out about now...

Fue admitido al Hospital de Santa María de las Hermanas de la Caridad de la ciudad de San Francisco, en el valle de la Yerbabuena, cuando cumplió treinta años, y fue diagnosticado con un síndrome de inmunodeficiencia adquirida en algún momento de su búsqueda ansiosa a través de algún fluido corporal que se escapó de entre las manos, de entre los testículos de su amante y penetró su piel y su flujo sanguíneo y lo llenó de un error fatal en el DNA, lo inoculó de una certeza de muerte temprana y de una incertidumbre de enfermedad y dolor que él se esforzó por entender en las explicaciones médico-virológicas de los doctores y los académicos, en la paradoja echada sobre su constitución química por un enemigo minúsculo, invisible y poderoso. Padeció tres años de abandono, deterioro y debilitamiento, y sintió su mente irse primero, y su apego a la vida seguirle. Leyó en algún lugar que un gran escritor y poeta había puesto su casa y sus libros en orden, había conservado sólo lo más querido e indispensable, y se había sentado a ver su sida traer su muerte. Y al poeta como a los muchos amantes, la muerte le llegó. Y se sintió culpable de estar vivo y triste de estar ya casi muerto. También tiró sus papeles, despreció a sus amigos, ordenó sus cosas y se acostó a morir con un toque de mota en la boca, con el humo del fuego interno que se apagaba nublándole la razón. Pero a los tres años se irguió de sus cenizas, se levantó de su lecho de muerte y contestó una llamada a la puerta de su casa. Era la ley que venía a tomar posesión de lo que le quedaba, incluso el espacio que ocupaba en ese país antes lejano y ajeno, ahora el único propio, pero todavía ajeno. Contestó a esa llamada con miedo primero, con indignación luego, y por fin vino la furia, y al enfurecerse, sintió su mente y su sangre volver a la vida, y esa sangre incompartible se le reveló fortalecida, impetuosa y hambrienta de amor y caricias, y esa mente enflaquecida por el largo ayuno luctuoso le quemó las sienes, y dejó atrás la cama de la muerte, llena de su miedo y fatiga, y se quitó de las manos los anillos y las pulseras que los hombres y mujeres de su vida le habían dado para usar, y se cortó el pelo largo, negro, que caía por sus hombros hasta la mitad de la espalda, y dejó que su cara delicada cuidada por los afeites y la sombra se embarneciera con la lluvia y el frío y el sol y el viento, y al crecerle barba por vez primera, la fuerza volvió a él, desde adentro y desde el fondo, y al llegar a la superficie se endureció alrededor de los músculos de la espalda, de los hombros, de las piernas, de los brazos, del pecho, y se admiró desnudo ante el espejo, y ese nuevo cuerpo le dijo que viviría. Le cerró la puerta de su casa a la ley, que no pudo llevarse lo que quería, y abrió las ventanas, y por allí entraron amantes de antes que eran en realidad nuevos amantes, pero también los que no regresarían nunca ya, y el calor de un beso tras la oreja, entre respiraciones entrecortadas, le hizo olvidar para siempre que había sido otro sin su supervirus y recordar para ya no olvidar que su vida y su muerte entraban con el aire fresco de ese largo fin de verano, de la mano. Muchos años después, al morir, sus restos fueron incinerados y llevados a Guayangareo, a la vieja Valladolid, donde fueron a descansar en los brazos amorosos de su abuela materna que lo estaba esperando, envueltos en el encaje negro rasgado de su velo luctuoso. Ahí yace, por fin en paz.

...because I have a now, a present, and a future that I am sketching on the old rags of yesterday with my new blood, blood with antibodies and protease inhibitors, blood of the pain I went through to accept this different chemical landscape inside me that, now I know, would be, is becoming, a new me all the time, in this land that is not mine, in this language that is not mine, in this time that is not mine but that I have reclaimed for myself from a place of no hope that we haven't been able to properly name, the time when we live and die with aids ...see, it is a conspiracy, it is a new way they're devising to keep us from our pleasures and our furtive happiness, I remember back then back home that's what they used to say, my friends, when this new specter rose in the early eighties in the little town with the little secret society of man-hunting lust that I belonged to, no, it can't be just that, there's got to be more to it than a simple, idiotic conspiracy by the keepers of the gates to normalcy, we had to find out more, and we did, when some started dying with deforming, debilitating, horrifying disease and pain, no, that can't be it, there's got to be more than a successful experiment at extermination, it's got to be us, with us, part of us, our own creature to understand and to grow with, it is not out there, it's in here and among us, it'll find its proper place and measure, as we have slowly understood, with time, after almost twenty years of the epidemic and half our address books blacked out, it is who we are, and we are what it is, this virus, which in the little town back then we couldn't even name, but some of us have remained so that the little town can now name us and not forget, so that we can name and not forget those crossed-out names and the world we shared at the end of innocence and the beginning of rubber between me and my sex, a world of survival paradoxes competing with love and pleasure, crossroads making us and the world all the more inscrutable... Which part of the paradox paralyzed us at the wrong turn? Did we choose, were we chosen? Is it a road, a path, a border between us and something else still elusive to us? Are these the questions of back then, still adolescents, or are they the questions of now, already a little too weary and a little too old to be asking them, a little too young to be survivors of the devastation?... They are simply the wrong questions, they pursue the mirage of certitude, when our only chance has been to ask time and again, to keep changing the questions, ahead of the brutal answers this disease would give us at each turn... Back in the little town I am asking myself these questions, unable to understand where they come from, who is drafting them for me, as I am now, when I have turned paler, when I have lost and acquired an accent, when I have embraced a language and relegated another one, and up on the surface of my skin the brown of my body embraces me, it alone, amid the whiteness, the pale colors of my sexile, of my desire, my acquired color-deficiency syndrome, my love of the white boy that bites into my earlobe as he says, I love you, and the dear old queens of my little town come back in a dream, the dead and the living, to tell me of their own sexiles and their own earlobe-biting boys as they watch me in these lands north of where our dreams were born, back then in the little town in the mother tongue, so far away from me as I embrace myself in this other language, land, smell, color, taste of me that wasn't me and is the only me now, even when I don't want it to be so, even when I resist it, even when this white world that violently adopted me by infusing in me a deadly virus rejects me at its borders because I am not pale enough still, because the mother tongue still insinuates herself when I want it, and when I don't, in the rhythms of the language in which I am loving and learning, growing and dying, with which I am struggling and winning, fighting and losing, because that pale desire is greater than me, because those barriers of whiteness are what I was born to measure up against, to lose against but at the same time to conquer as I have, as we all from the little town back then have to...

About the Authors

Francisco X. Alarcón, a Chicano poet and educator, teaches at the University of California–Davis. He has authored ten volumes of poetry, including *Body in Flames/Cuerpo en llamas* and *De amor oscuro/Of Dark Love*. Alarcón coauthored *Ya Vas, Carnal,* one of the first collections of homoerotic Latino poetry. His bilingual children's book, entitled *Laughing Tomatoes and Other Spring Poems/Los jitomates risueños y otros poemas de primavera* received the Pura Belpré Honor Award from the American Library Association. He has also been honored with a Fulbright Fellowship, the American Book Award, and the Chicano Literary Prize. He can be reached by email at fjalarcon@ucdavis.edu

D. L. Alvarez is a visual artist who writes. The child of biker parents Sharkey and Ethel, he grew up in Stockton, California. He has had solo exhibitions of his art in San Francisco, London, Paris, Naples, and New York City, and currently lives in Brooklyn.

Rane Arroyo, Ph.D., is a professor of Creative Writing and American Studies at the University of Toledo, Ohio. He is the author of numerous books of poetry, including *Pale Ramón* and *The Singing Shark*. He has received awards for both his poetry and playwriting, including the Carl Sandburg Poetry Award and the Pushcart Prize. His works have been published in *The Americas Review, Callaloo, Caliban, Kenyon Review,* and other publications. He has written several plays, including *Buddha and the Señorita, Emily Dickinson in Bandages,* and *Prayers for a Go-Go Boy*. He can be reached by email at rarroyo@pop3.utoledo.edu.

Pedro Bustos Aguilar was born in Morelia, Michoacán, México, on October 9, 1960. He graduated from the State University of Veracruz's Facultad de Idiomas with a double degree in English and French. He attended the University of Texas–Austin's doctoral program in Comparative Literature, to which he was admitted to candidacy in 1995. He lives with HIV in San Francisco, where, after a three-year hiatus, he is he is writing his dissertation on the Mexican gay and lesbian movement and its literature.

Ricardo A. Bracho is a writer, educator, and organizer who was born in Mexico City, raised in Culver City, California, and has made the San Francisco Bay Area his home for the past decade. He was the 1999 NEA/Theatre Communications Group playwright-in-residence at Theatre Rhinoceros. He also works in San Quentin Prison on the H.I.P. H.O.P. project (Health in Prison, Health Outta Prison).

James Cañón was born and raised in Ibagué, Colombia, and is the author of a number of short stories, including *The Two Miracles of the Gringos' Virgin* and *I Was Born That Way*. He is working on his MFA in Creative Writing at Columbia University. He is currently working on a novel set in Queens, New York, where he has lived since 1992. His work appeared in *Besame Mucho* (Painted Leaf, 1999). He can be reached by email at JAMESCANON@aol.com.

Raúl Coronado Jr. is a native-born Tejano who received his B.A. at the University of Texas–Austin. He is currently pursuing his Ph.D. in Modern Thought and Literature at Stanford University, where he is also "in exile." Along with being a fervent follower of the Selena phenomenon, he's been known to do drag. He can be reached by email at raulc@leland.stanford.edu.

Jorge Ignacio Cortiñas has been published in *Puerto del Sol, Socialist Review, Best Gay Erotica '98*, and *Modern Words*. He won first prize in the 1998 *San Francisco Bay Guardian* fiction contest.

His play *Maleta Mulata* was recently produced by the Campo Santo theater company in San Francisco. He is currently a Creative Writing Fellow at Brown University.

Jason Flores-Williams is a contributor to *Hustler, Prison Life,* and *Soma* magazines. His fifth novel, *The Last Stand of Mr. America* (Caught Inside Press, 1998), is excerpted in these pages. He is twenty-nine years old and lives in San Francisco.

Ramón García grew up in Modesto, California, and now lives in Los Angeles. He has a B.A. in Spanish Literature from the University of California–Santa Cruz and a Ph.D. in Literature from the University of California–San Diego. His poetry has appeared in *New Chicana/o Writing #1; Flight of the Eagle: Poetry on the U.S.–Mexico Border*; *The Americas Review*; *Poesída: An Anthology of AIDS Poetry from the United States, Latin America, and Spain*; and *Best American Poetry 1996*. His fiction has appeared in *Story*. He can be reached by email at RGarciaMon@aol.com.

Erasmo Guerra was born and raised in the Rio Grande Valley of South Texas. He has been published in the *James White Review* and the anthologies *New World: Young Latino Writers* (Delta, 1997), *Gay Travels: A Literary Companion* (Whereabouts Press, 1998), and *Men Seeking Men* (Painted Leaf Press, 1998). His work appears in *Besame Mucho* (Painted Leaf Press, 1999). He is the editor of *Latin Lovers: The Stories of Latin Men in Love* (Painted Leaf Press, 1999). He was a writing fellow at the Vermont Studio Center in the winter of 1998. He lives in New York City.

Al Lujan is a writer, visual artist, performer, and filmmaker. Raised in East Los Angeles, he now makes San Francisco his home. His artwork has been shown at Yerba Buena Center for the Arts, Galería de la Raza, Folsom Street Interchange, Four Walls Gallery, and Artist's Television Access. His writing has appeared in *Beyond Definition: New Queer Writers of San Francisco*; *Best American Erotica 1995*, *Best Gay Erotica 1997*, *Sex Spoken Here*, *Drummer* magazine, and the 'zines *A la Brava* and *Manteca*. He is a founding member of the queer Latino comedy troupe Latin Hustle. He can be reached by email at al_batross@hotmail.com.

Randy Pesqueira is currently an arts administrator at the Huntington Beach Art Center, a contemporary art space in California. After helping to organize and run two AIDS organizations in Orange County, he began writing and performing in various venues, including Highways performance space in Santa Monica. He resides in Garden Grove. He can be reached by email at randex@hotmail.com.

Horacio N. Roque Ramírez, a salvadoreño del Cantón Comecayo, is a Ph.D. candidate at the University of California Berkeley, where he is conducting an oral history study of queer Latina and Latino community formations in San Francisco. An immigrant by trade, he has taught in the social science department at San Jose State University. He can be reached by email at hnroque@uclink4.berkeley.edu.

Lito Sandoval was born in Woodland, California, and now lives in San Francisco. He cowrote and costarred in *Full Frontal Rudity,* a series of skits, with the queer Latino comedy troupe Latin Hustle. His poetry has appeared in *Prosodia*, *Xipactli*, *Whorezine*, and *A la Brava*. He can be reached by email at Elsand@aol.com.

Roger Schira is a native New Yorker who attended City College and The Neighborhood Playhouse. He is the author of several plays, screenplays, and short stories. His play *KUBA* was workshopped at South Coast Rep's Hispanic Playwrights Project and later at San Francisco's Latin American Theater Artists. His latest play, *The Puerto Rican Room,* was recently read at the Mark Taper Forum's Latino Theatre Initiative. He lives in Manhattan.

Raúl Thomas was born in Xalapa, Veracruz, México. He studied philosophy and literature in Mexico City and has lived in San Francisco since 1981. He is the author of *Las Caras de la Luna*, *Cincuenta Años de Amor,* and *Dicen Que Soy, y Aseguran que Estoy*, which is currently being considered as a film project by several directors.

Joel Antonio Villalón has written fiction that has appeared in anthologies, reviews, and newspapers. Born and raised in South Texas, he currently lives in San Francisco.

Emanuel Xavier crashed onto the literary scene with a self-published poetry collection entitled *Pier Queen.* His poetry has been published widely, and his short fiction has appeared in *Best Gay Erotica 1997, Men on Men 7,* and *Busame Mucho.* He is the author of a novel, *Christ-Like* (Painted Leaf Press, 1999). He co-stars in Henry B. Roas' independent film, *A Day in the Life* (forthcoming) and Emanuel can be reached by email at PAPIboy@aol.com.

Rodolfo Zamora is a twenty-six-year-old creative writing major at California State University–Long Beach. and plans to pursue a Master of Fine Arts program. His focus has been poetry, but his poems have been screaming to be written down in the short story form. He was lucky to have been born in Mexico when his parents were visiting there. While he was growing up, his parents moved around a lot from Northern California to Southern California, giving him the opportunity to live in obscure little cities like Pixley and Terra Bella.

About the Editor

Jaime Cortez is a visual artist, writer, and comic performer based in San Francisco's Mission District. He was raised by Felipe and Felisitas Cortez, farmworkers who migrated between Mexicali in Baja California and San Juan Bautista in Alta California. He attended Watsonville High School and the University of Pennsylvania, where he studied communications and English. He served for two years as a public high school teacher in Yamanashi Prefecture in Japan and has since remained in the nonprofit sector, working in the areas of AIDS and the arts. He is currently porgram manager at Galería de la Raza.

Though Cortez began editing publications at the age of thirteen, his first love is visual art, and his drawings and paintings have been exhibited at numerous galleries in San Francisco. In 1997, he cofounded the comedy group Latin Hustle. Jaime's work has been published in *Queer PAPI Porn* (Cleis Press), *2sexE* (North Atlantic Press), *Besame Mucho* (Painted Leaf Press), and his own 'zine, *A la Brava*.